No Friends for Hannah

Other Crossway Books by
Hilda Stahl

THE SADIE ROSE ADVENTURE SERIES
Sadie Rose and the Daring Escape
Sadie Rose and the Cottonwood Creek Orphan
Sadie Rose and the Outlaw Rustlers
Sadie Rose and the Double Secret
Sadie Rose and the Mad Fortune Hunters
Sadie Rose and the Phantom Warrior
Sadie Rose and the Champion Sharpshooter
Sadie Rose and the Secret Romance
Sadie Rose and the Impossible Birthday Wish

GROWING UP ADVENTURES
Sendi Lee Mason and the Milk Carton Kids
Sendi Lee Mason and the Stray Striped Cat
Sendi Lee Mason and the Big Mistake
Sendi Lee Mason and the Great Crusade

KAYLA O'BRIAN ADVENTURES
Kayla O'Brian and the Dangerous Journey
Kayla O'Brian: Trouble at Bitter Creek Ranch
Kayla O'Brian and the Runaway Orphans

DAISY PUNKIN
Meet Daisy Punkin
The Bratty Brother

BEST FRIENDS
#1: Chelsea and the Outrageous Phone Bill
#2: Big Trouble for Roxie
#3: Kathy's Baby-sitting Hassle
#4: Hannah and the Special 4th of July
#5: Roxie and the Red Rose Mystery
#6: Kathy's New Brother
#7: A Made-over Chelsea

Best Friends

#8

No Friends for Hannah

Hilda Stahl

CROSSWAY BOOKS • WHEATON, ILLINOIS
A DIVISION OF GOOD NEWS PUBLISHERS

Dedicated with love to
Carole Gift Page

No Friends for Hannah.

Copyright © 1992 by Word Spinners, Inc.

Published by Crossway Books, a division of
Good News Publishers, 1300 Crescent Street, Wheaton, Illinois 60187.

Cover illustration: Paul Casale

First printing, 1992

Printed in the United States of America

Library of Congress Cataloging-in-Publication Data
Stahl, Hilda.
   No friends for Hannah / Hilda Stahl.
      p.   cm. — (Best friends : #8)
   Summary: After God answers her prayers by giving her three new
best friends, twelve-year-old Hannah worries because they are suddenly
too busy to stand by her, at a time when she is facing prejudice against
her because she is an Ottawa Indian.
   [1. Friendship—Fiction. 2. Christian life. 3. Ottawa Indians—
Fiction. 4. Indians of North America—Fiction. 5. Prejudices—
Fiction.] I. Title. II. Series: Stahl, Hilda. Best friends : #8.
PZ7.S78244No 1992   [Fic]—dc20   92-13272
ISBN 0-89107-684-0

00		99		98		97		96		95				
15	14	13	12	11	10	9	8	7	6	5	4	3		

Contents

1

Too Busy

Smiling, Hannah rushed outdoors past the mob of middle-school students to catch the Best Friends and ask them over for pizza. This morning Mom had said she could. She wanted to have a sleepover, but Mom had said it was too hard with baby Burke still so young. Hannah frowned. Sometimes having a baby brother was terrible.

Just then she saw the Best Friends talking together in the shade of a tree near the row of buses. Chelsea McCrea held a camera as she laughed at something Roxie Shoulders had just said. Roxie swung her tennis racket, almost hitting Kathy Aber. Hannah hesitated. Did they even notice she wasn't with them and that she hadn't joined any of the clubs?

Hannah shrugged. She wanted the Best Friends to be happy, and they really were. Students shouted and laughed. Smiling, Hannah ran down the steps into the boiling sun. Sweat dampened her skin, making her jeans stick to her legs. She brushed back her long, dark hair. For the first time in her life she had friends—best friends. Before this past summer nobody had wanted to get to know her because she was Ottawa. With her wide forehead, high cheekbones, and black hair and eyes she couldn't hide her heritage even if she wanted to—which she didn't. She was proud to be Native American, even though sometimes it was hard because of people's prejudice.

"Hi, girls." Hannah thankfully stepped into the shade.

"Hi!" they all said together.

"It's almost too hot to do anything." Roxie fanned herself with her tennis racket.

"That's for sure!" Chelsea lifted her long red hair off her neck.

Kathy twirled and grinned. "Who cares if it's hot!"

Hannah took a deep breath. "Could all of you come to my house now for pizza?"

"Sounds great . . . except . . ." Chelsea looked down at her camera. ". . . I have a meeting, and then I'm going to Kesha's." Kesha was a new friend of Chelsea's, and they both belonged to the Photography Club.

Hannah's heart sank. It wouldn't be fun without Chelsea.

"I have cheerleading practice." Kathy twirled around, making her short skirt flare out.

Hannah laced her fingers together. How can you have a party with only two people!

"And I have a game, even if it is hot." Laughing, Roxie swung the racket. "I'm playing with Betsy. She thinks she's sooo good!"

Hannah's smile faded. *None* of them could come! They talked about their plans as if they didn't even feel bad about missing a pizza party at her house! Slowly she walked away. She thought they'd call to her and ask where she was going, but they didn't. She glanced back. They were talking and laughing and didn't even notice she was gone! Tears burned her eyes. She'd thought they were different, but maybe . . . She told herself they were just too busy right now, that they still wanted her for a friend. She'd call them tomorrow and invite them over then. They'd probably have more time on Saturday. She blinked her tears away and ran for the bus.

Saturday morning Hannah stretched the phone cord as far away from the noise in her kitchen as she could so Chelsea could hear her. "Chel, could we go to the park this morning?"

"Oh, sorry, Hannah! Not this morning! Kesha and I are going to take pictures for the photo contest."

9

Hannah's heart sank. Kesha again! "Well, maybe I'll call Kathy or Roxie."

"Kathy's practicing cheerleading, and Roxie already went to the tennis courts for a game with another girl."

Hannah sighed. "Well, okay. I'll talk to you later. Have fun taking pictures."

"Thanks. We will."

Slowly Hannah hung up. Was it possible the Best Friends had dropped her? Didn't they like her anymore? She shook her head. They were just too busy for her. That had to be it. It would be awful if they dropped her—too awful for words!

Taking a deep, steadying breath, Hannah turned to face the usual noise of Saturday morning breakfast. The eight-year-old twins Vivian and Sherry were arguing over who would get the toy inside the cereal box, nine-year-old Lena was trying to talk Mom out of taking her to her piano lesson, and Mom was feeding baby Burke a gooey mixture of oatmeal and bananas. He spit out the bite, but Mom caught it with the spoon and poked it right back into his mouth. Dad stood with his head in the refrigerator, looking for peach jam. He wore his usual Saturday clothes—faded jeans and a plaid shirt.

"Isn't there any peach jam left?"

"It should be on the door," Mom said.

He turned and grinned, the jam held high. "If it was a snake, it would've bit me."

Hannah didn't laugh like she usually did when he said something like that.

He cocked his dark brow. "What's wrong, Hannah?"

She struggled to hold back her tears. "Chelsea can't go with me. She's too busy. So are Roxie and Kathy. It's been that way ever since school started last week."

Dad slipped an arm around her and pulled her close to his side. "You'll have to find something else to do. It doesn't do any good to feel sorry for yourself . . . And it's a waste of time."

"I know."

"When you're feeling down, help somebody in need. That'll perk you right up."

Hannah sighed. Dad had been telling her that as long as she could remember. And he was right! But this time she didn't feel like doing something for someone else. She wanted somebody to do something for her, to take away the pain she felt because the Best Friends were abandoning her.

"Hannah, could you take the twins to the park this morning?" Mom wiped Burke's mouth, then held him to her shoulder to burp him.

Dad reached out and took the baby. Mom frowned slightly, but didn't say anything.

Hannah's nerves tightened. She'd noticed Mom

11

had been upset a lot lately because of all the time Dad spent with the baby. He sometimes ignored Mom and talked to the baby. Hannah knew Mom didn't like that at all.

Mom leaned her elbows on the table and looked up at Hannah. "Will you, Hannah? I have to take Lena to her piano lesson."

Hannah didn't want to take the twins to the park, but she also didn't want to make Mom feel any worse than she already did. "Sure . . . I'll take them."

Lena jumped up and ran over to Mom. "I want to go to the park too! Please *please* let me skip piano."

Mom chuckled as she tugged on Lena's shoulder-length black hair. "Lena, it's your first lesson. You can't skip your very first lesson. And you'll be going for the next several years, so get used to it."

Hannah bit back a laugh. She'd taken piano since she was nine, and she still wanted to skip lessons. She'd practiced regularly all summer but hadn't had lessons because her teacher was away. Next Saturday she'd start again. When Lena got a little older, maybe they'd have the same teacher.

Dad pushed his face into baby Burke's neck. "You and I will stay home and play."

Mom frowned. "Be sure you let him sleep, Chief."

Hannah stood very still at the sound of Mom's sharp voice.

"Don't worry, Beryl." Dad kissed Burke's cheek. Dad's name was Burke also, but from the time he was in high school folks had called him Chief. "I smell a smell, my boy, and that tells me you need changing."

"I can change him," Mom said.

"I'll manage." Dad grinned at Burke. "Won't I?"

Hannah leaned weakly against the counter. She'd never felt tension between Mom and Dad before baby Burke had come along. Hannah watched Dad walk out of the kitchen and heard his boots clomp on the stairs. The nursery used to be her bedroom, but now she had a bedroom in the basement with Lena and the twins. The entire basement was theirs. So far it had been great. She didn't know how it would be when the girls got older.

Several minutes later Hannah followed the twins out into the bright morning sunlight. The smell of freshly cut grass filled the air. Trees lined the streets of The Ravines, the subdivision they'd moved into two years ago. Flowers bloomed in almost every yard. Hannah wiped sweat off her face. Mom had said it might rain later today, but right now it was almost too hot to breathe. Hannah tugged her blue shirt over her shorts. A movement near a bush at the side of the house caught her attention. She looked closer. It was Gray, the huge gray cat that belonged to Tom and Julie Wirt, the neighbors in back of them. The Wirts usually kept the cat in the house, and when they let him out they put a leash on him. But there was no leash on the gray cat now.

"Wait, girls!" Hannah motioned to them. They turned to see what she wanted. They were identical twins in looks only. Vivian was noisy and Sherry quiet. They both wore yellow shorts and white T-shirts. "Look over there!"

"It's Gray. I'll get him!" Her braids jumping around her thin shoulders, Vivian raced after the cat. It yowled and ran across the yard toward the tall rock near the sidewalk.

"Don't chase him!" Sherry cried, waving her arms. "You'll scare him. Let me catch him."

Hannah rolled her eyes. She'd have to do something or they'd never get to the park. "Vivian, come here. You're scaring the cat."

Vivian made a face at Sherry, then ran over to Hannah. They watched as the cat stopped near a patch of red flowers and Sherry crept toward him.

"Kitty . . . Nice kitty . . . Come to me, Gray." Sherry talked softly as she walked closer and closer to the big gray cat. She bent down and touched Gray. He meowed but didn't leap away. Carefully she picked him up. He filled her arms and looked too heavy for her. She grinned triumphantly at Vivian, then walked to the row of bushes that separated the two yards. She easily walked between the bushes and disappeared from sight.

"She thinks she's sooo big because she can catch that dumb cat and I can't." Vivian tossed her head, and her braids jumped. "She's not so big! I could catch Gray too if she'd leave me alone and let me do it my way."

Hannah pulled Vivian close to her side. She smelled the apple shampoo Vivian had used to wash her hair. "Some things you do better, and some things Sherry does better. That's the way it should be. Gray is afraid when you run at him. Sherry knows that."

"I guess." Vivian lifted her dark eyes so she could look at Hannah. "It's just that most everything Sherry does is better than me."

Hannah smiled and shook her head. "That's not true. You run faster. You do better in gym."

"I know." Vivian sighed heavily. "I wish I could do *everything* better than her!"

"Then she'd feel bad all the time. You wouldn't want that, would you?"

Vivian shrugged. "Well, I don't know . . . No, I guess I wouldn't."

Just then Hannah caught a glimpse of a face peeking around a tree in the Wirts' yard. The face disappeared as quickly as it had appeared. Hannah shivered. "Who's home at the Wirts'?"

"Nobody." Vivian shook her head. "They go to work early, even on Saturdays."

"I'm sure I saw somebody."

"It's probably the wicked witch Sherry told me about."

Shivering again, Hannah frowned. "What wicked witch?" She hadn't heard Sherry mention any such thing.

"She says there's one living in the Wirts' little barn." Vivian lowered her voice almost to a whisper. "But I looked and there's not. Sherry only made it up to keep me from going over there when I'm not supposed to."

"Probably so." Hannah bit her lip. The Wirts had built a little red barn in the corner of their yard and used it for a toolshed. She looked for the face again. It had come and gone so suddenly, it was probably just her imagination.

Smiling, Sherry ran through the bushes and up to Hannah and Vivian. "I put Gray back inside the porch." She frowned and rubbed at her damp face. Cat hair clung to her T-shirt. "The door was unlocked. I bet Tom will yell at Julie for leaving it unlocked. I heard him yell at her before."

"Don't worry about it." Hannah tugged Sherry's braid. Hannah had heard Tom yell at Julie too, but she didn't want Sherry to be concerned or frightened about it. "Let's go to the park before it rains."

Vivian made a face at Sherry. "I could've caught Gray if you had let me."

Sherry shook her head. "Could not!"

"Cut it out, girls!"

Arguing, the twins dashed away, leaving Hannah behind. She stayed behind them all the way to the park so she wouldn't have to listen to their fights or their constant chatter. In the park she wiped sweat off her face while the twins drank from the fountain. Shouting, they ran to the swings. The fight was over. Hannah bent over the fountain. The cold water felt good against her lips and in her mouth. She swallowed. The water soothed her dry throat and took away the taste of dust.

Slowly she walked to the green bench, sat down, and watched the twins. She was glad their fights never lasted long. Before long they ran from the swing to the merry-go-round. Then after a few minutes they ran to the sandbox. Hannah moved restlessly. It was very boring just watching them. She walked to the sandbox and squatted down beside them. "Can I play with you?"

"No." Vivian shook her head.

"We're telling secrets." Sherry leaned against Vivian and giggled.

"I'd like to hear a secret," Hannah said, smiling.

"No way!" The twins shook their heads hard.

Hannah bit her lip. The twins didn't want her around any more than the Best Friends had.

Slowly Hannah walked back to the bench and sat down. She felt just as lonely as she had before Chelsea moved into the house across the street from her and they'd become friends. Maybe it was time to face the truth—she didn't have any friends anymore. A lump lodged in her throat, and tears pricked her eyes.

2

Still Too Busy

Her raincoat over her arm, Hannah waited just inside the church while Dad brought the car around. Rain pelted against the pavement, leaving puddles here and there. The church was almost empty. It usually took Mom a long time to get Burke out of the nursery and ready to take home. Carrying Burke, Mom walked down the wide hall with the twins and Lena. Mom was talking to Billie McCrea, Chelsea's mom. Hannah glanced past them to see if Chelsea was coming. Surely today on such a rainy day the Best Friends would come over for pizza! She'd asked them in Sunday school, and they'd told her they had to ask their parents.

Just then Hannah saw Chelsea and Kathy walking slowly down the hall, talking excitedly. Hannah hurried up to them. She took a deep breath. "Did you ask?"

Chelsea looked up. "Oh, hi, Hannah." Chelsea

nodded. "I asked, but Mom says we're going out to dinner and then I have homework. Sorry."

Hannah tried her very best not to feel sad, but her heart sank anyway.

Kathy wrinkled her nose. "We're going to Aunt Patty's for the afternoon. After that I have homework too. Sorry, Hannah."

"Me too," Hannah whispered. She cleared her throat so she could talk without sounding like she'd burst into tears. "How about Roxie?"

"She'll be gone too." Chelsea slipped her tan jacket on over her blue-and-white dress. "She said to tell you she'd talk to you in school tomorrow."

Hannah nodded. Once again the Best Friends were too busy for her. The lump in her throat grew so large she couldn't speak as the girls hurried out the door into the rain. Biting back a moan, Hannah slipped on her raincoat.

"Hannah, help the twins to the car," Mom said as she eased her hood over her head.

Hannah herded the twins out the door after Lena and into the back door of the station wagon. Cold wind blew against her. Rain soaked through her shoes and dampened her legs.

"Don't touch me!" Lena moved away from the twins. "Mom, Sherry got my skirt muddy!"

"Girls!" Dad frowned over his shoulder. "Sit still and be quiet. Sherry, keep your feet off Lena's skirt."

Sherry burst into tears.

Hannah turned her face to the window and watched the rain-streaked cars whiz past. She wished she could cry like Sherry. But she wasn't eight like Sherry—she was twelve and in sixth grade at Middle Lake Middle School.

A few minutes later Hannah followed the family out of the garage and into the house. Smells of roasting chicken and scalloped potatoes filled the house. Hannah breathed deeply. Her mouth watered.

"Girls, change your clothes and hurry to the kitchen." Mom started upstairs with Burke. "Chief, will you check the chicken?"

"Sure will!" Whistling, Dad hurried to the kitchen.

Hannah ran downstairs, pulling off her clothes as she did. She hung her clothes in the closet that stretched from one corner to the bathroom door. It was big enough for all four girls, with shelves to hold odds and ends. It smelled like cedar. The basement walls were paneled with oak, and the floor was covered with soft gray-and-blue carpet. Part of the room was a playroom for the little girls. Shelves full of stuffed animals and brightly dressed dolls stood under two windows. A weak light shone through the windows. Hannah slipped on jeans and a red short-sleeved sweatshirt that felt snug and warm. She pulled on red socks and white sneakers.

The twins giggled and chattered as they changed into jeans and sweaters. Lena stood beside her bed and looked sad and lonely. Finally she changed into jeans and a green sweater.

"Stop it, Sherry!" Vivian stamped her foot. "You're making that up!"

"Stop fighting," Lena snapped.

Vivian turned to Lena and Hannah. "Sherry said she saw the wicked witch at the Wirts' again."

Sherry crossed her arms and lifted her chin. "Well, I did! So there! I saw her standing behind a tree, and she was teasing Gray."

Lena jabbed Sherry's arm. "Stop making up stories! You know what Mom said."

Sherry ran to the stairs. She stopped at the first step and looked back. "I'm telling the truth! I mean it!" She dashed upstairs, her braids flipping across her back.

Hannah shivered. Was Sherry telling the truth? She sometimes did make up stories, but she always admitted it when she did.

"She's still mad because I finally caught Gray yesterday," Vivian said, giggling.

"Did you chase that cat?" Hannah frowned at Vivian.

She shrugged and giggled harder. "I said I could catch him, and I did. We don't know how Gray got out again. Sherry said the old woman let him out. I sure don't believe that."

"Why don't you ever let me do things with you?" Lena pushed her face right up to Vivian's. "I want to know about Sherry's story! I want to help catch Gray!"

Vivian shrugged, then ran for the stairs.

Hannah sighed. "Let's go, Lena."

She hung back and shook her head. "Do you ever wish you had a twin?"

"I guess . . . Sometimes."

"I don't have anybody to tell secrets too. I'm too old to tell my teddy bear." She flung her arm toward the worn brown teddy bear on her bed.

"Hey, you can tell me." Hannah smiled and squeezed Lena's hand. She hated to see Lena so alone all the time.

"You're always too busy with your best friends."

Hannah bit her lip. Maybe not anymore, but she didn't tell Lena that. "Let's go eat."

Lena's chin quivered, and her dark eyes filled with giant tears. "Hannah, will I ever have a friend?"

"Does God answer prayer?"

Lena nodded.

"That's your answer."

Lena knuckled away her tears and dashed up the stairs.

Hannah hesitated, then followed, clicking off the light as she walked past. God did answer prayer!

He'd given her three best friends. But what if they didn't want her any longer?

She pressed her hand to her stomach and moaned. Oh, that couldn't happen! It just couldn't! She rushed to the dining room and helped set the dining room table. They mostly ate dinner in the dining room, and always on Sundays.

She stood back and looked at the flowered plates, tall glasses filled with ice water, silverware that Sherry had set just right, and folded yellow napkins. The table was set for six, but it could seat twelve with all the leaves in it. A tall china cabinet stood against one wall and a buffet against another. An old-fashioned china pitcher sat inside a huge china bowl on the buffet. Sometimes Mom filled the pitcher with flowers. Today it was empty.

Hannah stood at the window and looked at the Wirts' yard. Through the bushes she saw the side of the small red barn with the tan roof. What had happened that led Sherry to make up a story about an old witch living in the barn?

Vivian ran to Hannah and peered out the window. "Do you see the old woman?"

"No."

Vivian turned and put her hands on her waist. "Sherry, you made up that story, didn't you?"

Sherry lifted her chin and looked smug. "I'm not telling, and you can't make me!"

With a platter of chicken in his hand, Dad

walked into the room just in time to hear what Sherry said. Steam rose from the chicken, sending out a delicious aroma. He set the platter near his plate, then swatted Sherry's bottom. "Don't talk sassy! Tell your sister you're sorry."

Sherry ducked her head. "Sorry," she whispered.

Vivian ran to Sherry. "I know . . . I forgive you."

Hannah smiled. The twins were always quick to apologize and to forgive. She wished Lena was. Lena sometimes did naughty things to the twins but had a very hard time saying she was sorry. Hannah could understand why. Many times she'd felt the word "sorry" stick on her tongue and it just wouldn't budge.

Mom carried in steaming potatoes and a bowl of buttered corn. "Hannah, get the rolls, would you?"

Hannah hurried to the kitchen. Dirty pots and pans covered the counter beside the basket of hot rolls. She picked up the basket and started toward the dining room when she saw a movement outside the window. Her heart in her mouth, she gripped the basket and peered out the window. She saw the small brown dog Gracie dash across the grass, barking like crazy. Mike McCrea was taking care of Gracie while Roxie's grandma and Ezra Menski were on their honeymoon in Hawaii. They'd be back later that week. Mike didn't want to give up Gracie, but he had to. Mike was eight and was proud that he could work for the *King's Kids*, a group of kids who did odd jobs for pay.

Hannah looked once more around the yard, then hurried to the dining room. She saw Dad and Mom smile at each other as she set the basket near the butter. The tension she'd felt when the family was together earlier slipped away. She sat in her chair, thankful to see Dad and Mom smiling at each other instead of frowning. Maybe it helped to have Burke asleep in his crib. The monitor sat on the table beside Mom's plate so she could hear if he cried.

Dad asked the blessing, served the twins and Lena some chicken, and passed it to Hannah.

Hannah carefully put a large piece of brown meat on her plate. She held the platter while Mom took a piece of white meat. Little baby noises came through the monitor.

Dad spooned potatoes and corn onto his plate. "Ginny called yesterday."

Hannah stiffened. Ginny had stayed a few weeks with them during the summer so Dad could help her with her drinking problem. Ginny was Dad's brother's daughter and *very* spoiled.

"How is she?" Mom asked as she took the corn from Hannah.

"Doing very well." Dad smiled at Hannah.

"She said she's been reading her Bible every day like you told her to do, Hannah."

"Good." Hannah sat up straight. Ginny had hated her when she'd first come, but by the time she left, they were friends.

"I wrote her a letter," Lena said. "Did she say she got it?"

Dad nodded. "She said she'll write. She wants you to write again."

Lena looked pleased.

Hannah took a bite of potatoes and savored the delicious taste of cheese and butter mixed in with the potato.

Suddenly something hit the window, and Hannah jumped.

"What on earth!" Mom ran to the window and looked out.

"It's probably that old woman," Sherry said as she carefully buttered a roll.

Vivian raced to the window and pressed her nose against it. "Is she there?"

Mom turned with a scowl. "No one's out there."

"I always miss her!" Vivian lifted her hands and let them fall to her sides. "How come you're the only one who can see her, Sherry?"

"Because she's not real!" Lena snapped.

Sherry took a bite of her roll and shrugged as if she couldn't care less what Lena thought.

Hannah narrowed her eyes. Maybe Sherry wasn't making up a story after all. Was it possible someone lived in the little barn?

Excitement leaped inside Hannah. Right after dinner she'd call the Best Friends and tell them she had a real mystery to solve. Then she remembered that they wouldn't be home, and even if they were, they had homework. They didn't have time to listen to her or help her solve a mystery. Her heart sank right down to her sneakers.

Listlessly she broke a roll in half and buttered it. Could she even solve a mystery if the Best Friends weren't around to listen to her discuss it?

3

The Old Woman

Hannah dropped her book on the floor beside her and sighed heavily. Sundays didn't usually seem so long, but today was stretching on and on. After she'd helped with dinner dishes she'd counted the money in the *King's Kids* treasury. There was five dollars—not much at all. They'd decided the *King's Kids* would work only on Saturdays and one evening a week now that school had started. During the summer they'd worked as often as they wanted. Chelsea was the president because she'd started *King's Kids*. Each person who worked gave 2 percent of his or her earnings for expenses or for a gift to someone in special need. Hannah kept the money in a special bag in her drawer.

Maybe Chelsea would get so busy with school and photography that she'd drop *King's Kids*. Hannah bit back a moan. That couldn't happen! She glanced at Lena sprawled across her bed reading.

The twins were watching a video upstairs in the living room. Mom and Dad were resting while Burke was asleep.

Hannah sat on the edge of her bed. "Want to play a game, Lena?"

She jumped up. "Yes! What game?"

"I don't care. Any game."

Lena ran across the room and leaped on Hannah's bed. "Wait . . . I know something better!" Her eyes sparkled and she looked ready to fly.

"What?" Hannah laughed. She liked to see Lena excited.

"It stopped raining. Let's go see if there really is someone living in the Wirts' little barn!"

"Oh, Lena!"

"No, really, it would be so much fun! Come on, Hannah!" Lena tugged on her arm. "You're the one who loves to solve mysteries. Let's solve this one. Please please please *please*."

"Oh, okay." Laughing, Hannah slid off her bed. "It'll be fun." A shiver trickled down her spine. It was wrong to trespass, but they weren't going to make any trouble, so wouldn't it be all right? Besides, the Wirts didn't care if they walked in their yard. She saw Lena's sparkling eyes and made up her mind. They would go—but they wouldn't stay long.

Lena giggled and twirled around and around, then dashed up the stairs. She waited until Hannah caught up with her. "We won't tell the twins, right?"

Hannah nodded.

"Not one word, right?"

"It's just between you and me." Hannah tickled Lena and made her giggle harder. "But we have to be very quiet or they'll hear us."

"But even if they hear us, they can't go with us, right?"

Hannah pushed her nose against Lena's and whispered, "Right."

Hannah led the way out the back door and into the yard. The air was cool and smelled clean after the rain. The grass felt spongy under her feet. The sun shone weakly overhead. She stopped at the row of bushes that separated their yard from the Wirts'. Someday the bushes would be so tight nobody would get through, but right now they were far enough apart that even an adult could slip between them. Hannah bit her lip. It still wasn't too late to back down.

Shivering, Lena caught Hannah's hand and held on tight. "What if there really is a witch?"

"There won't be."

"But what if there is?"

"If there's someone there, it'll be an ordinary person. You'll see."

Lena trembled. "Oh, it's so exciting."

Hannah thought so too, but she didn't say it aloud. She really did need to check out the little red barn for Lena's sake. It would be terrible if she thought there really was a witch living at the Wirts'. Her pulse racing, Hannah led the way to the small red barn and peeked through the side window. She saw a chair sitting in the middle of the concrete floor, a lawn mower, and a rake.

Lena stood on tiptoe. "I can't see! Is she in there? Hannah, I can't see!"

"Shhhh!" Hannah lifted Lena so she could see inside, then dropped her back onto the wet grass. "See? Nothing!"

"Maybe she's hiding in a corner." Lena hugged her arms against herself. "She could be! I want to look in the door."

"Lena, we can't! That's wrong, and you know it."

Lena looked toward the house. "I bet the Wirts aren't even home. And even if they were, they wouldn't care. Let's look real fast, then leave."

Hannah knew they should get back home where they belonged, but she really wanted to look inside too—especially after all the stories Sherry had told. It couldn't hurt to just look. They weren't going to steal or destroy anything. The Wirts had always welcomed them into their yard.

With Lena's hand in hers, Hannah ducked around the barn to the door. It had an open padlock hanging on it. She hesitated and then with trembling hands pushed the door in. The smell of potting soil drifted out toward them.

Lena ducked inside and looked around.

"Nobody's in here! I *knew* Sherry was making it up!"

Hannah hesitated, then stepped inside. Her head almost touched the rafters. Just then she spotted a paperback book under the white lawn chair. She shivered as she picked it up. It was a mystery novel. It had a bookmark on page 245. Carefully she put the book back under the chair. Why would the Wirts leave the book in the barn? Did one of them come here to read? Hannah shook her head. Nobody would leave the beautiful house and comfortable chairs to spend time reading in the red barn.

Wham! The door had suddenly closed! Lena cried out and grabbed Hannah.

"The wind probably blew it shut." Hannah shivered. *What wind?* She hadn't noticed any wind. And how could the wind blow the door when it was inside the barn? But what else would make the door close? Hannah turned the knob and pushed. The door wouldn't open. Her skin felt like it was being stabbed by a thousand very sharp icicles. She tried the door again. The knob turned, but the door wouldn't open. She remembered the bar and the padlock. Had someone put the bar and padlock in place?

"What's going on?" Lena's voice was weak, and she looked ready to cry. "I'm scared, Hannah."

"So am I," Hannah whispered through a dry throat. Oh, why had they trespassed? And who had

33

shut the door on them? She lifted her hand to knock, then dropped it at her side. It would be terrible if the Wirts came outdoors and found them in their barn.

Lena fell against the door and hammered on it with her fists. "Help! Open the door!"

Hannah reached to stop Lena, then dropped her hand. Lena was right—they had to have help to get out, no matter how embarrassing it was to be caught trespassing.

"We're inside and we can't get out!" Lena shouted.

Hannah peered out the window. She saw Gray amble across the yard and disappear from sight. Gray was out again without his leash!

Lena burst into tears and began pounding harder. "Let us out! Please let us out!"

Hannah heard a slight sound. She gripped Lena and shushed her. She pulled Lena tight against her and strained her ears for another sound. None came. Her heart was beating so loudly, she was sure her family must hear it.

"What's wrong?" Lena whispered.

"I thought I heard somebody." Hannah pressed her ear to the door and listened. Was that someone breathing just on the other side of the red door? She shivered.

Lena pressed her face against Hannah's arm.

"We shouldn't have come. I knew it!" Lena cried.

"You shouldn't have." The whispery voice came from outside.

Hannah gasped.

Lena fell against the door and pounded again. "Let us out!"

Hannah pulled Lena back. "Who's out there?"

No one answered.

Hannah sucked in her breath. Suddenly it seemed like there wasn't enough air in the small space. She gasped for breath, and her head spun.

Lena pulled away and rattled the knob. Surprisingly, the door moved, and she pulled it in. "It opened!"

Air rushed in, and Hannah breathed deeply. She leaped out after Lena and looked wildly around for the person who'd let them out. Was it the same person who had locked them in?

Hannah caught Lena's hand and raced over to their own yard. Would someone jump out from behind a tree and grab them? But nobody did. Hannah stopped in their yard and looked back. Nobody stood in the Wirts' yard. Not even Gray was in sight.

"It was the old woman," Lena whispered.

"Did you see her?"

Lena shook her head hard. "But I heard her."

"It could've been someone playing a trick. Maybe Chelsea's brother Rob."

"He wouldn't do that."

"I guess you're right." As Hannah scanned the Wirts' yard, she caught a glimpse of someone hiding behind a tree. "Who are you, and why'd you lock us in?" she shouted.

An old woman stepped from behind the tree. She wore a plaid dress that reached almost to her ankles and a rumpled purple hat on her gray hair. Her face was lined with deep wrinkles.

Hannah gasped, and Lena shrieked.

The woman shook her scrawny finger at the girls. "You stay away from my place!"

Hannah jerked Lena after her to their back door. The knob was cold to her touch, and for a minute she couldn't turn it. Sweat popped out on her forehead. Finally she got the door opened. She pushed Lena in first, then jumped in after her. She closed the door and leaned weakly against it. After a long time she looked out the window. The old woman was gone.

"Was she real?" Lena whispered.

"I don't know . . . Yes, she was."

"I'm telling Dad!"

"No!" Hannah shook her head. "We weren't supposed to be there, Lena. We can't tell anyone."

Lena scowled. "Not even the twins?"

"Especially not the twins! They'd spread the story around. Mom and Dad would hear, and the Wirts might find out we went in their barn. We can't tell anyone!"

Lena trembled, then brushed at her eyes. "I wish we didn't go there."

"Me too." Hannah leaned weakly against the wall. Who was the old woman? Why had she locked them in the barn? What if she told what they'd done? With a gasp Hannah jerked up and peered out the window again. She had to find the woman and apologize for trespassing, then beg her not to tell anyone.

"Lena, I gotta go back."

"No!" Lena's eyes grew big and round. "You can't! She might hurt you!"

Hannah's nerves tightened. Lena could be right. "I have to go anyway."

"Then I'm going with you!"

Hannah smiled. "Thanks."

Lena nodded and looked pleased with herself.

Slowly Hannah walked out again with Lena close at her side. A breeze cooled her hot skin. They hesitated at the bushes, then stepped into the Wirts' yard.

"We came to talk," Hannah called.

"We won't hurt you," Lena shouted.

Trembling, Hannah waited. Was the woman still in the yard? "Please talk to us!"

"Maybe she's gone."

"Maybe."

"I'm right here," the woman said sharply.

Hannah looked all around. She heard the voice but couldn't see the woman. "Will you talk to us?"

"No need! Just leave me alone."

"We want to apologize for trespassing."

"So you apologized—now go home!"

Hannah swallowed hard. "Don't tell our folks, will you?"

"I don't ever talk to anyone. Now leave me alone. And leave that gray cat alone. He wants to roam free. He doesn't want to be shut up in the house all the time."

"He belongs to the Wirts," Hannah said hesitantly.

"I know."

Hannah glanced at Lena, then off to where the voice was coming from. Why would the woman even care if Gray was inside or out? "Who *are* you?"

"None of your business."

"I'm Hannah Shigwam, and this is my sister Lena."

"I know. You're Ottawa Indians."

"How do you know?" Lena asked.

"I been watching all of you since I came here."

Hannah shivered. The woman had watched her and she hadn't even known it! "Do you live with the Wirts?"

"Of course. You think I'm trespassing?"

Hannah bit her lip. "We're sorry we did."

"I know. Just don't do it again."

"We won't!"

38

"We promise." Lena nodded hard.

"Don't talk to me again. I'm going inside."

Hannah watched but didn't see the woman. "I think she's gone," Hannah whispered.

"I'm scared!"

Finally Hannah walked through the back door with Lena. "I wonder who she is."

"Sherry'll find out."

Hannah gripped Lena's arm. "We can't tell the twins. Understand?"

Lena tossed her head and looked smug. "Sherry will find out anyway."

Hannah grinned. "I guess you're right. But until she tells us, we have to keep quiet."

"That'll be hard."

"I know." Hannah hugged Lena. "Let's go get something to eat, then play a game."

"Really?"

Hannah nodded. Lena ran into the kitchen, and Hannah followed. She glanced out the window. Had they really seen and talked to the old woman? Or had it all been a Sunday afternoon dream? Maybe she'd wake up and find herself in her own bed with her book beside her. She looked at Lena. She was taking ice cream from the refrigerator. She was real, not a dream character. Hannah groaned. The old woman was real—just as real as Lena! Hannah trembled.

4

Facing the Truth

The phone rang, and Hannah jumped, almost tipping over her glass of milk right onto the twins.

Lena leaped up. "I'll get it."

Stuffing the rest of her cookie into her mouth, Hannah raced across the kitchen, but Lena beat her to the phone on the wall and answered it breathlessly. Lena's face fell, and she handed the receiver to Hannah, then walked back to the table and the twins.

Hannah swallowed, made a face at Lena, then answered.

"Hi. It's Chelsea."

Hannah's heart leaped. It was late Sunday afternoon, and she'd thought she wouldn't hear from any of the Best Friends until tomorrow. "Hi, Chel! . . . Can you come over? . . . Can I come over?"

"Sorry, Hannah. I'm stuck on my homework."

Hannah sagged against the counter. "Oh."

"I got a call a few minutes ago for someone to work right after school tomorrow. Can you do it?"

"I guess so."

"Good!" Chelsea read off the information.

Hannah grabbed a pad and pencil and wrote fast.

"Did you get it?"

"Sure." Hannah looked at the scribbles she'd made. Later she'd copy it over so she wouldn't make any mistakes. She knew she didn't have to be concerned about the job or the employer. Chelsea or her dad always checked over the people who called for one of the *King's Kids*. Nobody worked unless an adult approved the employer. And nobody worked for free unless it was decided ahead of time. They did do good deeds regularly but only after they agreed on it. Hannah took a deep breath. "Chel, I have something really really exciting to tell you."

"Great! I'll talk to you on the bus or sometime in school tomorrow. Gotta go now. I promised Mom I wouldn't stay on long."

"Bye," Hannah said weakly. Slowly she hung up and walked back to the table. The chocolate cookies she and Lena had baked after they'd eaten ice cream suddenly looked and smelled terrible.

"What's wrong?" Lena asked.

"Nothing." Hannah carried her glass to the sink and poured out the leftover milk, then set the glass in the dishwasher. She'd desperately wanted to run to Chelsea's house to tell her about the old woman.

"Do you have a *King's Kids* job?" Lena picked up the scribbled note.

Hannah scowled and jerked the note away from Lena.

"Can I help you do it?"

"No. Chelsea said it's a one-person job."

Looking sad, Lena leaned against the counter. "I want a job too. Why can't I go with you?"

"You just can't." Hannah forced back her anger. It wasn't right to take her frustrations out on Lena. "But I'll remind Chelsea you're on the list and that you want a job."

Lena smiled, then turned to the twins. "I get to work and you don't."

"Do too!" Vivian made a face. "I'll tell Chelsea to add my name to the list. I can do the same work you can." She turned to Sherry. "Right, Sherry?"

She nodded. "There's two of us. We can do real good work!"

Impatiently Hannah walked out of the kitchen, leaving the twins and Lena arguing over who could do better work. The smell of the chocolate cookies followed her into the living room. Mom and Dad were watching TV. Baby Burke lay in his little bed at Dad's feet. Before they even noticed she'd walked in, she slipped out and hurried to the study. She could call Roxie or Kathy and tell them about the old woman.

Hannah sat at the desk and tried Roxie first. Her sister Lacy answered.

"Roxie's not home. I think she's at Chelsea's house."

Hannah's stomach knotted. Before she could ask Lacy more, Lacy hung up. Why would Roxie and Chelsea be together and not want Hannah there? Maybe Lacy was wrong.

Hannah waited a minute, then called Kathy. There was no answer. What if Kathy was at Chelsea's too? Would the Best Friends meet without her?

Shaking her head, Hannah jumped up. They wouldn't do that to her! They were her friends—her very best friends!

The next morning at school Hannah looked for the Best Friends. She spotted them in the homeroom, but just then the tardy bell rang, so she couldn't talk to them. Just after reading, she caught up with Chelsea in the hallway on the way to math. Noise echoed up and down the hall. The odor of dirty socks blended together with the smell of grape gum.

Hannah caught Chelsea's arm. "Wait'll you hear, Chel!"

"Have you seen Kesha?" Chelsea flung back her red hair and looked up and down the hallway.

"She said she'd bring my math book. I left it at her house by accident."

Hannah bit her lip and dropped her hand to her side. "Don't you want to hear my news?"

"Sure . . . but not right now. Oh, there's Kesha! See ya later, Hannah." Chelsea hurried away, waving at Kesha.

Slowly Hannah walked to math class. She saw Kathy talking to Alyssa and Debbie, two of the cheerleaders. Roxie came in right when the tardy bell rang. She didn't even look at Hannah.

Hannah sank low in her seat and opened her math book. She had to face the terrible truth—the Best Friends didn't have time for her. She didn't have any friends. A loneliness washed over her, leaving her feeling weak and sad. Before she'd had friends she'd felt lonely, but this was worse because for a time she'd had someone to talk to and share secrets with and now she didn't!

Tears welled up in Hannah's eyes and blurred the problems in her math book. She blinked, and a tear plopped down and left a wet mark on the page. Quickly she brushed at her eyes and forced back the tears. She would not cry!

At lunch Hannah deliberately sat at a table with girls she didn't know. She almost choked on the corn dogs and the tiny container of vanilla ice cream. Voices rose and fell. A chair crashed over, and someone shouted. Smells of pizza, corn dogs, and tomato soup filled the room.

Just then a blonde girl with glasses said, "Aren't you Hannah Shigwam?"

"Yes." Hannah's stomach knotted. Was the girl going to tell her the only good Indian was a dead Indian?

"Weren't you one of the winners of the red rose art contest last month?"

Hannah nodded, her hands quiet in her lap. What was the girl going to say next?

"Why aren't you in the special art class on Tuesdays?"

"I never even thought about joining." Hannah didn't want to say that she'd been turned away from many activities in the past just because she was Ottawa and didn't want to be turned away again.

"Well, I think you should join." The blonde girl smiled and pushed up her glasses. "I'm Brianna Cobb."

Hannah smiled, surprised Brianna would even suggest that she join the art class. "I might check into it."

"There's room for only a few more, so you better do it today. You can sign up at the office."

"Thanks." Hannah watched Brianna wad up her white paper napkin. "Did you enter the art contest?"

"Sure did." Brianna rolled her eyes. "I didn't

have a chance, but I entered anyway. I'll keep entering and keep learning. One of these days I'll win!" She smiled and walked away.

Hannah thought about that as she finished her ice cream. She'd never keep trying like Brianna had. It wasn't worth being hurt over and over.

A few minutes later Hannah walked slowly down the crowded hallway to the office. She might as well sign up for the art class. So what if they wouldn't take her? She'd try once but only once.

She heard a laugh and looked over her shoulder. Chelsea was laughing at something Kathy and Roxie had said. What was so funny? Why hadn't Chelsea called to her and told her too? But she knew why. Tears burned her eyes, and her heart ached. She was no longer a Best Friend. They didn't have time for her. They didn't even want her! As soon she got home she'd throw away her *I'm A Best Friend* button.

At the office Hannah waited in line behind two boys who were talking about getting passes to leave class early. They glanced at her and then turned quickly away. She bit her lip to hold back a moan. Two women standing behind the office desk were taking care of the students. A phone rang, and a man at another desk answered. Finally Hannah reached the desk. She swallowed hard. She tried to smile but couldn't. Did she even want to sign up for art class?

"Could I help you?" the woman asked impatiently.

Hannah cleared her throat. Her jeans and short-sleeved yellow top felt too hot. "I'd like to sign up for the Tuesday art class please."

The woman looked through her papers and then turned to the woman beside her. "Jane, do you have the sign-up sheet for the Tuesday art class?"

Jane looked and shook her head. "Sorry, Tess. Maybe it's full."

Tess turned back to Hannah. "The class is full. You should've signed up last week."

"But Brianna Cobb said there were still openings." Hannah moved restlessly. Why even bother to say more? "Is there another place I could go to sign up?"

Tess frowned. "We'd have the sheet right here. Your friend is obviously wrong. Please step aside."

Hannah trembled as she slowly walked out of the office. The shouts of the students and the banging of the locker doors seemed extra-loud. The lights shone down brightly on the boys and girls. Hannah looked toward the outside door and wished she could leave school right now and go home. But she knew she couldn't. She'd have to go to classes, then ride the bus home the same as usual.

Just then Brianna Cobb ran up to Hannah and smiled. "Did you sign up?"

Hannah stiffened. Was Brianna playing a cruel

joke on her? "I tried, but they said the class was full."

"But it's not! I was just talking to Miss Norville, the art instructor. I told her you might be coming to class, and she was glad."

"Maybe she doesn't know it's full."

"She said she'd just checked and it wasn't." Brianna frowned. "I don't understand. Come on, I'll go to the office with you."

Hannah hesitated. "That's okay. We'd better get to class before we're late. Do you have English right now?"

"No . . . P.E.." Brianna looked at her watch. "We have time, Hannah. Let's go to the office. Come on . . . I'll go with you."

"I don't know . . ." Hannah looked toward the office just as a boy walked out and headed right for them. He stopped beside Brianna. He was medium build and wore faded jeans and a gray sweatshirt with the number 151 on it.

"Hi, Bri. I got in."

"Great, Todd!" Brianna smiled. "This is Hannah Shigwam. She was one of the winners in the rose contest last month."

"Hey, great!" Todd smiled. "I entered, but I didn't win. You in Tuesday art class?"

Hannah shook her head, then hooked her long hair behind her ears. "They said it's full."

Todd frowned. "But I just this minute signed

up. And I saw on the sheet there's room for three more students."

Hannah's legs suddenly felt too weak to hold her. It had happened again! She'd been kept from a special class just because she was Ottawa!

Brianna caught Hannah's arm and tugged hard. "Come on—sign up right now and you'll get in!"

Shaking her head, Hannah pulled free. "I changed my mind." Biting back a whimper, Hannah hurried toward English class. Would she ever be accepted like everyone else?

5

Hannah's Job

Hannah rang the doorbell, then waited. The two-story white frame house with an orange door belonged to Paula Mercer, the woman she'd be working for. The front yard was quite large, with toys scattered here and there. A dog yapped nearby, and from inside the house children shouted. Chelsea had said Mrs. Mercer wanted the children's playroom cleaned. That shouldn't take very long. Hannah rang the bell again. Maybe she should've brought Lena with her to help keep the children entertained.

Suddenly the door opened, and a girl about six years old stood there. She wore pink shorts and T-shirt and had a sucker in her mouth. She pulled the sucker out of her mouth with a loud *pop* and frowned. She had two teeth missing. "What d' you want?"

Hannah smiled. She'd been around obnoxious

kids before. It was best to ignore them. "Is your mom home?"

"Sure." The girl didn't move.

"I'm Hannah Shigwam. She's expecting me."

"So?"

Hannah wanted to jump on her bike and pedal home. The Mercers lived two blocks outside The Ravines. "Please tell your mom I'm here." The girl still didn't move. "Right now!"

The girl stuck her tongue out at Hannah, then raced away yelling, "Mom, there's a dumb girl at the door!"

Hannah groaned. She was really glad she was cleaning, not baby-sitting. She peeked inside the hall. Clothes and toys were scattered on the floor. A black scuff mark ran from just inside the door to the living room carpet. The smell of buttered popcorn drifted past her, making her mouth water. She loved popcorn! She'd eaten a peanut butter and peach jam sandwich with a glass of milk before she left for the job, but the popcorn made her hungry again.

After a long time Paula Mercer came to the door, brushing her long brown hair. She wore a pretty flowered dress and high-heeled shoes. "Hi, Hannah. Come in. And please call me Paula. I never answer to Mrs. Mercer."

Hannah hurried after Paula, who stopped in the bathroom and motioned Hannah to follow. Paula finished her hair, put on her makeup, then

51

studied herself. Hannah moved restlessly. The smell of perfume made her throat itch.

"Now, Hannah, I'll show you the playroom. Clean it first, then the rest of the house. After that, the yard. Don't let the kids make a mess. We have four kids—Elise, six; Rita, five; Sam, three; and baby Aaron, who's four months old today. Be sure Rita and Sam are in bed by 8:30 and Elise by 9. The baby will want a bottle in about a half an hour, then should sleep all the time I'm gone. If he doesn't, then just carry him in the baby pack while you work. He likes that."

"Gone?" Hannah's head whirled at all the work Paula expected her to do, plus baby-sit. "But I can't stay late!"

"But of course you can! Call your parents and get permission before I leave."

"Leave?"

Paula patted Hannah's arm. "I'm meeting my husband after work, and we're going out for the evening."

Hannah helplessly shook her head. "But I came to clean, not baby-sit. I can't do both."

"But of course you can!" Paula smiled. Her bright red lips stretched across her well made up face. "I'll be glad to pay you extra."

"Well . . . Okay." But was it really okay? Could she clean and baby-sit four kids? "I really should call someone to help me."

"That's not necessary at all." Paula hurried to the kitchen, picked up her purse and car keys, then started for the door. "You'll find the kids in the playroom and the baby in his crib. See you later."

"Wait . . ." Hannah watched the door close. Helplessly she stood at the window and watched Paula drive away in her small red car. Finally Hannah walked to the phone. Popcorn was scattered across the counter and on the tiled floor. She lost all hunger for popcorn. Sighing heavily, she called home and told Mom what had happened.

"Paula Mercer shouldn't have left you all alone. But I'm sure you can manage. If you have any problems, call me and I'll get Chelsea to send help."

"Thanks, Mom." Just then something crashed to the floor upstairs, and a child screamed. "Mom, call Chelsea right now and have her send someone. And tell her to hurry!"

Hannah hung up and ran in the direction of the noise. She finally found the kids in the playroom upstairs. A large wooden rocking horse lay on its side in the middle of the disaster area. Elise, the girl who'd answered the door, tugged on the horse's head while Rita pushed on its rump. Crying at the top of his lungs, Sam stood back against the empty toybox. Hannah wanted to run to her bike and ride home. How could Chelsea send her to a place like this? Well, she was here, so she'd better take charge!

"Let me help," she shouted over the noise. Sam

stopped crying and stared at her. The girls backed away from the horse and stared at her too. She flushed. Why were they staring at her that way?

Elise looked past Hannah to the door. "Where's Mom?"

"I want my mom." Rita popped her thumb into her mouth and sucked it hard.

Hannah picked up a big stuffed rabbit. They didn't even know their mom had left! Hannah stiffened. Now what would she do? She smiled and held up the pink gingham rabbit. "Where does this go?"

"We want our mom!" Elise stamped her foot and crossed her thin arms.

"She'll be here before you know it. Let's clean the room and surprise her. She'll walk in and say, 'Did my dear children clean the playroom? How wonderful!'"

"She wouldn't say that!" Elise pulled the rabbit out of Hannah's hand and tossed it to the floor.

Hannah's temper shot right through the ceiling, but she refused to let Elise know. Oh, how long would it take for Chelsea to send help? Hannah listened for the doorbell even though she knew it was too soon for help to come. She couldn't just stand and wait! She'd have to do something. Silently she asked God to help her know how to handle the kids while she did the work she'd agreed to do.

She rubbed her hand down the horse's saddle. "Whose horse?"

"Mine," all three kids said.

Hannah smiled. "Sam, do you want to ride him?"

Sam sniffed and barely nodded.

"I get to ride first!" Elise ran to the horse and climbed on.

Sam burst into tears and yanked on Elise's leg. "My turn! My turn!"

Rita tugged on the horse's rope tail. "I get to ride! It's my turn!"

Hannah lifted Elise to the floor before she had a chance to kick and scream. "Nobody can ride the horse until the room is clean."

Sam tried to climb on, but Hannah pulled him off. With the kids screaming and shouting, she pushed the horse into a walk-in closet and closed the door. She stood with her back against the door and looked sternly at the kids. "It won't do any good to scream or shout. You can't ride the horse or even touch the horse until this room is clean. If you keep crying or yelling, you won't get a turn at all. I mean every word I say!" She watched them think over what she'd said. Finally they stood quietly in the middle of the room. "Elise, you pick up all the stuffed animals and put them where they belong." Hannah glanced quickly around. She saw a big net hanging in a corner. "Put all of them in the net." Hannah turned to Rita. "Pick up all the dolls and set them on the shelf over there. And, Sam, you put the trucks and blocks in the toybox."

As the kids worked, Hannah noticed a broom and dustpan in the corner. Paula had probably put them there to sweep up the popcorn that had been spilled in there too. With a quiet sigh Hannah started picking up the books at her feet. Soon she could see the once highly polished wood floor. With all of them working together the toys were soon picked up. Hannah swept the floor, and Elise brought the wastebasket so they could dump in the dustpan full of popcorn.

"Now we'll get out the horse."

The kids clapped and shouted happily.

Hannah pulled the horse out of the closet. "Sam first. Rita and Elise, come help me while Sam rides. We'll have fun cleaning the house." Oh, where was the help Chelsea was sending?

Elise ran into her bedroom and picked up stuffed animals and set them on the shelf.

Rita climbed on the bed and jumped up and down in the middle of it.

Hannah caught her and moved her to the floor. "Pick up all the clothes and put them in that basket." Hannah pointed to the white plastic basket next to the closet door.

Just then the baby cried from a room down the hall. Hannah sank weakly against the wall. How could she feed the baby and still take care of everything? Where in the world was the help Chelsea was sending? Hannah bit her lip. The first free minute she had, she'd call and ask.

In the nursery Hannah lifted the baby from the crib. He was about the same size as baby Burke. His skin and hair were light instead of dark like Burke's. She changed his diaper and threw the dirty one in a diaper pail lined with a white plastic bag. The smell rose up and almost knocked her off her feet. The bag was almost full of soiled disposable diapers. She'd make sure she carried them out and put a new bag inside the pail.

She found a full bottle on the dresser. Hannah sat in the rocking chair and stuck the bottle in the baby's mouth. He sucked hungrily. He was soft and cuddly just like baby Burke. She listened for sounds from the other kids but didn't hear anything. They were quiet—too quiet. Her heart lurched. What if they messed up the playroom again? She wanted to check on them, but she had to sit quietly to feed the baby so he wouldn't get an upset stomach. Mom had told her that.

Finally, when Aaron quit sucking, Hannah set the bottle down and lifted him to her shoulder to burp him. She carefully stood up, patting the baby's back the way Mom had taught her. She walked down the hall, looking in each room. The girls weren't in Elise's room. They weren't in the playroom either. Hannah's heart sank. The kids weren't upstairs at all! Her stomach knotted. Just where were they and what were they doing? Now she had a better idea of how Kathy had felt when her little sister Megan was missing last summer.

"I will never work here again," she muttered as she rushed to the nursery. She grabbed the bottle and walked downstairs as quietly as she could. She found the kids in the living room watching a cartoon on TV. *Thank You, Jesus.* Hannah silently walked away. Mom would never let the twins or Lena watch that particular cartoon show, but Hannah figured Paula didn't care which programs her kids watched.

Wearily Hannah sat in the kitchen and finished feeding Aaron his bottle. She burped him again, then carried him upstairs to his bed. Just as she started out of the room, he cried. Her shoulders drooped. The baby cried harder. Pressing her lips tightly together, she found the carrier and strapped it on, then carefully tucked Aaron in it with his head against her heart. She'd work this way until he was asleep.

Downstairs Hannah peeked in the living room again. Another cartoon was on, and she left before the kids spotted her. She hurried to the kitchen and called Chelsea. Her mom answered and said Chelsea wasn't home. "Do you know if she sent someone to help me?"

"I really don't know, Hannah. Sorry."

"When will she be back?"

"By 8."

Hannah bit her lip. "I really really need help."

"If she said she'd send someone, then she did. She wouldn't forget."

"I know. Thanks, Mrs. McCrea." Hannah hung up and leaned weakly against the wall. Maybe she should call Mom to see if Lena could come help. But Lena was only nine and not old enough to do all that needed to be done. Besides, Mom wouldn't let her stay up late on a school night.

Sighing, Hannah cleaned the kitchen. She found a note on the refrigerator that told what the kids were to eat for dinner. Her heart sank. How could she fix them something to eat? But she couldn't let them go hungry. She opened the can of spaghetti, then poured it all into a microwave bowl and heated it while she quickly made cheese sandwiches. She ate a half a sandwich while she worked. She poured milk for the kids to drink. When she had it all ready on the table, she called them. Shouting, they ran into the kitchen and right to the table. They ate as if they were starving.

"I'll put the baby to bed and be right back." Hannah smiled, but the kids didn't even look up. She hurried upstairs and carefully put the baby in his crib. Thankfully he stayed asleep. She looked longingly at the rocking chair. She'd like to sit down and stay there until Paula came home.

Hannah took a deep breath and ran back

downstairs to the kitchen. Sam had red sauce all over his face, on the table, and on the chair he was sitting on. His glass lay on its side, and milk ran down the table onto the floor. Tears of frustration pricked Hannah's eyes, and she looked longingly toward the door. Where was her help?

"I'll get you more milk, Sam." Hannah poured a small amount of milk into his glass and held it out to him. He took it, smearing her fingers with red sauce.

"Sam doesn't know how to eat without making a mess." Elise looked very smug. "Me and Rita do."

"You sure do!" Hannah smiled. They'd finished their food and had only a little sauce on their faces. She gave them cookies and more milk, then cleaned up Sam's mess. She started the dishwasher, then sent the kids to the backyard to play. It was fenced in and had a huge swing set and a sandbox with a roof over it. While they played in the backyard, she cleaned the rooms downstairs. She couldn't find the vacuum cleaner, so she didn't vacuum, but she did dust.

She looked at her watch for the millionth time. "Chelsea's not sending help. If she had, they'd be here already. I'm leaving! I don't care what happens to those kids—I'm leaving!"

Hannah made a face. Who was she kidding? She couldn't just walk away and leave the kids all alone.

At 8 she fed the kids bananas, then sent them all to bed. She read a story to each of them. She almost fell asleep herself when she was reading to Elise.

Finally Hannah walked downstairs. She was going to sit on the couch and stay there until Paula got home! Hannah looked out the window. Toys were still scattered around the front yard. Tiredly she walked out and carried the tricycles into the garage. She took the balls and trucks to the playroom. Just as she got back downstairs Paula came home. She looked happy and rested and excited.

"Hannah, you did a wonderful job! My husband won't be home until later, and he has the money. You go on home, and I'll pay you tomorrow."

Hannah's heart sank. One of the *King's Kids* rules was to collect the money when the job was done. "I really need the money now."

"I don't understand why."

"It's a rule. I have to collect my pay now."

Paula's face hardened. "Well, I'm sorry, but I don't have it. My husband does. If you want to be paid, come tomorrow and I'll give it to you."

Hannah was too tired to argue. "I'll come right after school tomorrow." She got on her bike and pedaled home.

Just as she got home she saw someone in the yard. "Chel!" Hannah ran

"Hi, Hannah." Chelsea smiled as if she was glad to see Hannah.

"I worked for Paula Mercer, and she made me do lots of work and baby-sit too. How could she do that to me? Does she always do that to the person she hires?"

Chelsea flushed. "I . . . I didn't check her out."

"What?"

"I was sooo busy, I just didn't do it!"

"Oh, Chel!"

"I know I should've checked her out."

"That's right. And you were supposed to send help. I waited and waited for someone to help me. Nobody came."

Chelsea frowned.

"My mom called you and asked you to send someone to help me. You told her you would."

Chelsea gasped. "Oh, Hannah! I forgot! I completely forgot! I'm sooo sorry!"

Hannah's eyes filled with tears. "It was really really awful, Chel."

"I'm sorry, Hannah."

"And she wouldn't pay me!"

"What?"

"She said I have to go back tomorrow to get the money."

Chelsea shook her head. "That's awful!"

"It was more than awful!"

"was my evening! I mean, you wouldn't

believe the trouble I had getting the right angle for my camera shot!"

Hannah bit her lip. Chelsea wasn't sorry at all! She was thinking only about herself! "Good night, Chelsea," Hannah whispered.

"See you tomorrow."

Slowly Hannah walked across the street and into her house.

6

Hannah's Pay

Hannah punched her pillow and tried to block out Lena's snores. How could Chelsea not check out Paula Mercer? And how could Chelsea forget to send help? Hannah punched her pillow again. Chelsea wasn't even worth having for a friend!

Just then the stair door opened, and a crack of light shone down the steps.

Hannah sat up in bed to see who was coming down. It was Dad. His feet were bare, and he wore his jeans and a T-shirt. He smiled at her as he sat on the edge of her bed.

"Mom told me what happened tonight. I wanted to make sure you were all right."

"I guess I am." She leaned her head against his arm. He smelled as if he'd just taken a shower.

"Why aren't you asleep yet?"

"My head just spins and spins!"

"You're tired." He put an arm around her and

64

held her to his side. "But don't go to sleep still angry at Chelsea."

Hannah stiffened. "But she was sooo bad to me!"

"No matter what someone does to you, you must forgive them and not be angry. That's what Jesus said."

Hannah sighed. "I know. But, Daddy, sometimes it's hard to do."

"Jesus will help you." Dad kissed Hannah good night and then walked silently upstairs.

Hannah flung herself back on her pillow. Why should she forgive Chelsea? Hannah squeezed her eyes shut tight. She knew why. It was hard to obey Jesus, but she would anyway. "Jesus, with Your help I forgive Chelsea, and I'm not mad at her anymore." A peace settled over Hannah, and she smiled. She pulled the sheet and cover to her chin and drifted off to sleep.

The next morning at school Hannah spotted Chelsea at her locker. Hannah hurried through the noisy crowd of students to tell Chelsea she wasn't angry, but before she reached Chelsea, Brianna Cobb caught her arm. Brianna pushed her glasses up on her nose. A wide blue barrette held back her blonde hair. She wore a yellow plaid blouse and black jeans.

"Hannah, there's time to go to the office right

now to sign up for art. Come on—we'll go together."

Hannah hesitated. Should she try again? No! She didn't want the pain. "Brianna, it's really nice of you to help me and to want me in class, but I don't want to try to get in."

"But why? You're so good!"

"Thanks." Hannah smiled weakly. She didn't want to explain to Brianna about prejudiced people, so she pulled free and hurried to class.

All day Hannah tried to speak to Chelsea, but she never could. She tried to sit with her on the bus, but the seat was full. When they got off the bus at The Ravines, Chelsea ran ahead and wouldn't look back even when Hannah called to her. Hannah frowned. Was something wrong with Chelsea?

At home Hannah changed into her jeans and blue top, ate a banana, then pedaled to Paula Mercer's house. Once again the front yard was full of toys. Frowning, Hannah rang the doorbell. The front yard looked as if she hadn't even cleaned it. Why didn't Paula have her kids put the toys away when they finished playing with them? That's what Mom did with the twins and Lena. A cocker spaniel ran into the yard and sniffed a tricycle.

The door opened, and Elise stood there with a sucker in her mouth. She pulled it out with a loud *pop*. "My mom said to tell you she forgot to get the money. You'll have to come back later."

Hannah's muscles tightened. "What time?"

Elise shrugged and started to close the door.

Hannah caught it and pushed her way inside. "Tell your mom I want to talk to her."

"She won't talk to you."

"Go tell her I won't leave until she does." Butterflies fluttered in Hannah's stomach. She had every right to collect her money.

Elise dashed away shouting, "Mom, she won't leave! Mom, she wants to talk to you! She won't leave!"

Hannah stepped around a truck and looked into the living room. It was as messy as it had been yesterday! Why couldn't the kids keep their things in the playroom?

Just then Paula marched down the hall. She wore jeans and a red sweater. "Just what are you doing in here? Elise told you I don't have the money."

Hannah trembled. She hated to be yelled at. "What time should I come for my money?"

"About 6."

"I'll be here."

Paula jerked open the door. "Next time don't come in unless you're invited! That's trespassing, you know."

Hannah stepped out onto the porch, and Paula slammed the door hard behind her. Hannah shivered. The cocker spaniel barked and ran away, its

HILDA STAHL

ears flapping wildly. Slowly Hannah walked toward her bike. She didn't want to return ever! The money wasn't worth the fight, was it?

She pedaled home and left her bike in the garage where it belonged. She'd been taught to do that since she was old enough to ride the tyke bike she'd had when she was two.

Just then Hannah heard loud voices in the backyard. She ran around the house and stopped short. Vivian and Lena were standing in the yard, looking toward the Wirts' yard and yelling, "Sherry, come back!"

Hannah caught Lena's arm. "What's wrong?"

Vivian burst into tears as Lena said, "That old witch got Sherry!"

Hannah gasped, and the blood drained from her face. "Why didn't you tell Mom?"

"She's taking care of Burke." Lena's voice broke. "What'll we do, Hannah?"

"We're scared!" Vivian wrapped her arms around Hannah and held on tight. "I want Sherry back! I want her back right now!"

Hannah took a deep breath and silently prayed for help as she pried the girls off her. "I'll get Sherry."

"But the witch will get you too!" Lena flung herself at Hannah and held on tight. Lena's black hair was damp with sweat.

68

Hannah bent down to Lena. "I'll be right back with Sherry. Let me go get her."

Vivian tugged on Lena. "Let her go. I want Sherry back."

Reluctantly Lena let go of Hannah and clung to Vivian. "Don't let her cook you and eat you," Lena said.

"Nothing will happen to me. I'll be right back with Sherry." Hannah lifted her chin and walked between the bushes into the Wirts' yard. A cold chill ran down her spine, and she wanted to turn back, but she continued on until she stood beside the little red barn. She peered in the window. The barn was empty. Fear pricked her skin. She'd expected to find Sherry in the barn. Where was she? Hannah wanted to shout to Sherry, but she didn't want the old woman to know she was in the yard.

Hannah walked around a flower bed and peeked behind a tree. She looked behind every tree, then ran to the front yard. Sherry wasn't there either. Finally Hannah walked to the back porch and opened the door. It squawked, and she jumped. Was Sherry inside the house with the old woman? A floorboard creaked, and Hannah stopped short. Blood roared in her ears. For a long time she couldn't move. Finally she forced her legs to work, and she walked across the porch to the door. She knocked, but the knock was so light she barely felt it on her knuckles. Taking a steadying breath, she knocked again, this time louder. Her knuckles hurt, and she rubbed them down her jeans.

The door opened, and the old woman stood there, frowning. She wore black slacks and a gray sweatshirt. "What are you doing here?"

"I came for my sister." Hannah's mouth was so dry, she could barely get the words out. "Is she here?"

"Why should she be?"

"My other sisters said she was." Hannah tried to see around the woman but couldn't. "Sherry! Are you in there?"

"Hannah!"

Her heart leaped, then plunged to her feet. The old woman wouldn't let her in! Hannah bobbed up and down and side to side to see around the woman. "Are you all right, Sherry?"

"I want to go home," Sherry said, bursting into tears.

Hannah shivered. "Let her go back with me."

"No!" The woman shook her head. A strand of gray hair fell over her wrinkled forehead, and she brushed it back with a wrinkled hand. "She walked over here, and she's staying!"

With shivers running up and down her back, Hannah shook her head hard. Her dark hair swished over her shoulder. "You can't keep her! My mom and dad won't let you!"

"Go back to your place where you belong." The woman started to close the door.

"Wait!" Hannah caught the door. "I want Sherry. Come here, Sherry!"

"I can't!"

Fear stung Hannah's fingertips. "Why can't Sherry go home with me?"

The old woman cackled. "I put a spell on her."

Hannah's breath caught in her throat. "I don't believe you!"

The old woman wiggled her fingers at Hannah. "Hocus-pocus." She bent down to Hannah. "One more word from you and I'll turn you into a toad!"

"Run, Hannah!" shrieked Sherry. "She means it!"

Trembling, Hannah shook her head and looked right at the old woman. "You don't scare me! You can't turn me or anyone else into a toad." Hannah lifted her chin high. She didn't want the old woman to know that inside she was shaking hard enough to turn her insides to slush. "Why are you doing this?"

The woman chuckled and shrugged. "Because your sisters think I'm a witch, so I thought I'd teach them a lesson."

"It's a cruel lesson! Now let Sherry out!"

The woman shrugged and stepped aside.

Hannah peeked around her. Sherry sat on a chair in plain sight. She was shivering, and her eyes were wide and wet with tears. "Come on, Sherry."

"If I move, she'll turn Vivian into a toad."

"Sherry, she will not! That's only make-believe. She just said that to scare you." Hannah held out her hand. "Now come on!"

Without taking her eyes off the old woman, Sherry slowly stood up.

"Well, get out of here!" the old woman snapped.

Sherry shot past her into Hannah's arms.

The woman shook her finger. "If you call me a witch, I'll act like a witch!"

"She's sorry," Hannah said. "They really know you aren't one. They thought it was scary to say it."

"Now they know." The woman stepped out on the porch and closed the door. "Did you get your money?"

Hannah frowned. "What money?"

"From Paula Mercer, of course."

"How do you know about that?"

"I heard you talk to Chelsea across the street. Did you get it?"

Hannah shook her head. "She said she forgot to get it from her husband and that I'll have to go back when he comes home tonight."

"She's giving you the runaround. She doesn't plan on paying you."

Hannah's stomach tightened. "How do you know?"

Sherry tugged on Hannah's arm. "Come on!" she whispered.

The woman shrugged. "I checked into her after I heard you and Chelsea talk. She does that with everybody who works for her. She has a hard time getting anyone to work for her more than once."

"But that's not fair! I worked really really hard. I should get paid!"

"You're right—you should."

"I'll get it at 6 when I go back." Hannah began moving off the porch with Sherry hanging on her.

"Nell Wirt."

Hannah turned back to the old woman. "What?"

"My name's Nell Wirt. I live here with my grandson and his wife."

"Oh!" Hannah smiled in relief. "Why didn't you say so before this?"

"I didn't want anybody bothering me."

"I'm sorry about the trouble we caused you." Hannah nudged Sherry. "Aren't we, Sherry?"

She barely nodded.

Nell crossed her arms and narrowed her blue eyes. "I lived by myself on my farm for more than twenty years. Then they said I couldn't live alone. They said I could live here with Tom or with my son George. He lives in Chicago. I sure wouldn't move there! So I came here with Tom and Julie."

Hannah didn't know what to say.

"It's boring as all get out. I read . . . putter around . . . sleep and watch TV."

"Can't you make friends?"

"Could if I wanted to, but I don't want to." Nell lifted her round chin. "I just want to be back on my farm."

"I'm sorry." Hannah didn't know what else to say.

"Let me know if Paula Mercer doesn't pay you."

Hannah stepped back in surprise. What did it matter to Nell Wirt? "Sure . . . I'll tell you."

"Fine." Nell walked back inside and closed the door.

Sherry trembled. "Is she a witch or not?"

"She's not! And you tell Vivian and Lena that. I mean it, Sherry!"

"I'll tell 'em."

"Let's go." Hannah ran home with Sherry.

Jumping and yelling, Vivian and Lena grabbed Sherry and hugged her hard.

Hannah looked thoughtfully at the Wirts' house. Why would Nell Wirt care if Paula Mercer paid her or not?

7

Another Try

Hannah trembled, took a deep breath, and rang Paula Mercer's doorbell. This time she'd collect the money! A warm wind blew the smell of freshly cut grass her way. A robin sang from a tall maple. She looked over her shoulder at the front yard. The toys were gone, and the lawn once again was tidy.

The door opened, and Paula Mercer stood there with a frown on her face. The smell of roast beef drifted out of the house. From the kitchen Elise shouted at Rita. Paula crossed her arms and tapped her toe. "Yes?"

For a second Hannah couldn't speak. "I came for my money."

Paula frowned. "What are you talking about?"

Hannah's heart plunged to her feet. Nell Wirt had been right! "You said to come back about 6 and you'd give me my pay for yesterday."

Paula shook her head, and her brown curls

danced on her slender shoulders. "I don't know where you got that idea. You didn't do all the work, so I refuse to pay you."

Hannah's mouth dropped open. She'd worked herself so hard she could barely walk!

"You didn't vacuum, and you didn't get the black mark off the tile right here behind me."

Hannah's mouth turned cotton-dry. "I worked hard. You know I did!" Her voice broke, and she forced herself to continue. "I want my pay."

"You don't deserve it, and I'm not paying you!" Paula slammed the door before Hannah could stop her.

Hannah stood on the porch a long time, her legs unable to move. Tears blurred her eyes, and she blinked them away. Finally she walked to her bike and pedaled home. Just as she reached her driveway she spotted Nell Wirt standing beside the big rock in the front yard.

"Well?" Frowning, Nell stepped toward Hannah.

Hannah stopped her bike and helplessly shook her head.

"I knew it!" Nell smacked her fist against her palm. "What an injustice!"

Hannah twisted her toe in the grass. "She said I didn't finish my work, so she doesn't have to pay me."

"You tell your friend Chelsea not to send anyone else there to work."

"I'll tell her."

Muttering to herself and shaking her head, Nell walked away.

Hannah bit her lip. It didn't make any sense for Nell Wirt to be upset. Hannah wheeled her bike into the garage. It smelled like motor oil in there. Both the station wagon and the small sedan were parked in place. She glanced back out the open garage door just as Chelsea walked into her own yard. Hannah hesitated, then ran across the street.

"Chelsea . . ." Hannah called, her mouth dry.

Chelsea turned slowly. Her face was red, and she looked upset. "Hi," she whispered.

"I just wanted you to know I'm not mad at you."

Chelsea sighed in relief. "Oh, Hannah, I'm so glad! I thought you were. I tried to talk to you in school, but you wouldn't look at me." She brushed a tear off her lashes. "I was so sure you were mad."

Hannah shook her head. "I was afraid you were." Then she didn't know what to say. She thought about one of the rules about making friends—"ask about the other person instead of just talking about yourself." "Did you get the pictures taken for the contest?"

Chelsea nodded with a big smile. "I think

they'll turn out great. They're being developed now. I'll get them tomorrow."

"How about Kesha's?"

"She said hers should be good. We neither one know if we have a contest winner, but I sure hope so." Chelsea flipped back her long red hair. "Did Paula Mercer pay you?"

"No."

"What? She didn't? But that's terrible!"

"I know." Hannah told Chelsea what Paula had said about not paying her and why.

"We'll get her to pay you! I mean it, Hannah!"

She smiled. It made her feel good just to hear Chelsea say that.

"The Best Friends will discuss ways at our next meeting."

Hannah tensed. Gracie barked in the backyard. A car drove past slowly, leaving behind the smell of exhaust. "When *is* the next meeting?"

"I don't know. Kathy can't do it today, and Roxie can't tomorrow. But we'll meet the first chance we can."

Hannah looked down at her feet, then up at Chelsea. "I was afraid I wouldn't be in the group any longer."

Chelsea's eyes widened in shock. "Why?"

"Because all of you have been too busy for me."

"Oh, Hannah! I'm really really sorry. We'll always be friends, no matter how busy we are."

"But it takes time, Chel. That's one of the rules you gave me: 'Take time for your friends.'"

Chelsea grinned. "I guess I forgot that rule, didn't I?"

Hannah nodded. "'It's hard work to make friends, and it's even harder to keep friends.'" Hannah giggled. "That was on your paper about making friends too."

"I remember. My mom told me that one. She said people get so involved with themselves that they forget about others. I don't ever want that to happen to us!"

"Me neither." Hannah's eyes sparkled. "I've got some really exciting things to tell you."

"I have to go in now." Chelsea flushed and giggled. "Sorry, but I really do. I'll talk to you tomorrow—for sure!"

"Okay." Smiling, Hannah said good-bye and ran back home. She'd wanted to tell Chelsea about Nell Wirt, but that would have to wait.

The next day after school Hannah stood in her yard. Should she go to Chelsea's house to talk to her? They hadn't been able to in school. Before she could make up her mind Mom called her in.

Frowning slightly, Hannah ran to the door. What had she done to upset Mom?

Her hand at her throat, Mom stood just inside the front door. "Paula Mercer just called."

"Does she want me to go get my pay?"

Mom shook her head. She rested her hands on Hannah's shoulders. "Paula Mercer said you tore up her yard and waxed her windows."

Hannah's knees shook, and for a minute she couldn't speak. "No way, Mom! I didn't do it!"

"I didn't think so, but she was so sure."

"I'm not the only person who was angry about not getting paid. I heard she's done that to other people who've worked for her. Maybe one of those people did it."

"Maybe. But she's telling everyone you did it." Mom pulled Hannah close and held her quietly for a while. Finally she kissed Hannah's cheeks and let her go. "I'm glad you didn't do it. I was sure you hadn't, but I had to hear you say it."

Hannah nodded.

Just then Burke cried, and Mom hurried away.

Hannah walked slowly to the kitchen. Here was a real mystery to solve. Maybe the Best Friends could work on it together.

Hmm. Who had waxed Paula Mercer's windows and tore up her yard? Maybe Nell Wirt knew.

Hannah dashed outside and into the Wirts' yard. She looked in the little red barn first. Nell sat inside reading a book. "Hi," Hannah said.

Nell looked up in surprise. She closed the book

and stood up. Her green dress reached almost to her ankles. "What are you doing here? I didn't invite you."

"I know." Hannah quickly told Nell what Mom had said. "So . . . I thought you might know who did it."

"How would I know?" Nell chuckled. "Serves her right, though, doesn't it?"

"She thinks I did it! I don't want others to think I'd do such a terrible thing."

"Paula Mercer probably did it herself."

"No! I never thought of that possibility."

Nell held up her mystery book. "I've been reading these since I was your age. I'm good at solving mysteries."

Hannah took a step forward. "Want to help solve this one?"

Nell's face brightened. "Yes! I just might solve it myself since I have more time to work on it than you do."

Hannah smiled. She'd never seen Nell look excited about anything. Maybe solving the mystery would make her feel better about being away from her farm. "I'll tell you what I learn, and you tell me what you learn, and we'll solve it together."

Nell nodded. "It's a deal."

Hannah stepped out into the sunlight, and Nell followed. "I don't know where to begin."

Nell puckered her brow and tapped her book against her hand. "How about Chelsea?"

"What about her?"

"Maybe she did it to get even with Paula Mercer for what she did to you."

"No." Hannah shook her head hard. "No. Chelsea wouldn't do anything to get even. She's a Christian, and she wouldn't do that."

"Not all Christians obey God's Word."

"Chelsea does," Hannah said firmly.

Later Hannah sat in Chelsea's bedroom and told her what had happened.

"I already heard." Chelsea chewed on her bottom lip. "Paula Mercer called me."

Hannah saw Chelsea was having a hard time saying what she had to say. Hannah's stomach knotted. "And?"

Chelsea looked down at her carpet, then at Hannah. "She said she'd post an ad in the paper and send flyers around telling everyone not to hire any of the *King's Kids* if I didn't take you off the list." Her eyes wide, Chelsea held out her hand. "But you know I won't do that! She's wrong. I know you did a good job for her, and I know she didn't pay you."

Hannah shivered. "Maybe I should quit *King's Kids* to keep from causing trouble."

"No way! That's the last thing you should do!"

"I don't want to make trouble."

"Tomorrow the Best Friends will meet and

decide what action to take." Chelsea lifted her chin, and her eyes flashed.

Hannah's heart leaped. It was Best Friends to the rescue once again! But could they solve the mystery in time to stop Paula Mercer from ruining the reputation of the *King's Kids*?

8

The Best Friends

With Chelsea and Roxie beside her, Hannah stood behind a giant oak and watched Kathy walk to Paula Mercer's door. Several shallow holes dotted the front lawn. Clumps of grass stood in piles near the ruined flower bed. Three windows had a thick, almost straight line of paraffin wax across the bottom. Who had done it?

Chelsea and Roxie whispered together, then were silent. Hannah shivered. They'd planned just what they were going to do, but would it work?

Kathy rang the doorbell and waited.

Paula Mercer opened the door. She wore jeans and a blue sweater. "Yes?"

Kathy squared her shoulders. "I'm looking for a part-time job to help pay for school clothes. Do you have any work for me to do?"

Paula frowned thoughtfully. "I don't know."

Hannah stiffened. They'd expected Paula to put Kathy right to work.

Chelsea lifted her camera, focused it on Paula and Kathy, and clicked a picture. "Got it," she whispered.

Hannah and Roxie smiled and nodded.

"I work hard and fast," Kathy said.

"Where do you live?" Paula asked.

"On Kennedy Street."

"I thought you lived in The Ravines."

Chelsea nudged Hannah and whispered, "She wants to make sure Kathy's not a *King's Kid*."

Hannah nodded.

"Does it matter that I don't?" Kathy asked.

"Not at all!" Paula smiled. "Can you work right now?"

"Sure. But only for a couple of hours. Me and my family go to church tonight."

"No problem. You can easily be done on time. Come in and meet my children."

Hannah watched Kathy walk inside and saw Paula close the door. Hannah turned to Chelsea and Roxie. "Wait and see if she doesn't drive away in just a few minutes."

Grinning, Chelsea lifted her camera. "I'm ready."

Roxie frowned as she peered around the oak. "How will we help Kathy without the kids telling on us?"

"If we act like we belong there, they won't think a thing about it." Hannah giggled. "If we do just what we talked about, it'll work."

"If Paula leaves, that is." Roxie brushed a twig from her short brown hair. "If she doesn't, what's Plan B?"

Hannah giggled. "Kathy works by herself."

"Did you notice the waxed windows?" Chelsea clicked a picture of one.

Hannah nodded. "They're only waxed at the bottom—like someone short did it. And the holes in the yard are shallow—like someone weak did it."

Just then the garage door opened, and Paula backed out her car. Chelsea clicked a picture, and then Hannah tugged the girls around the tree and out of sight. Paula drove away, leaving behind exhaust fumes. Hannah ran with the girls into the open garage and through the connecting door into the laundry room. It smelled like wet diapers. Hannah led the way upstairs where she was sure they'd find Kathy. Elise and Rita were yelling, and Sam was crying. How could the baby sleep through it all?

With a laugh Hannah walked into the messy playroom. Kathy looked ready to run away. "We're here, Kathy." Hannah turned to the kids who immediately grew quiet. "Hi, kids. I came to work together with you again. Isn't that great?"

Elise looked uncertain. "My mom didn't say you were coming."

"It doesn't matter. Sam, put the trucks and blocks in the toybox." Hannah gave orders while Chelsea clicked pictures.

Baby Aaron started crying, and Kathy hurried away to tend him with Chelsea on her heels to take more pictures. After that Chelsea and Roxie would go outdoors to clean the yard, try to scrape the wax off the windows, and take even more pictures. The photos would be the proof of the good work the *King's Kids* did, as well as proof they had indeed worked at Paula Mercer's.

In an hour the entire house was cleaned and the baby back to sleep. Her head high, Hannah walked to the kitchen to meet the Best Friends. She gave the kids apple and cheese slices and then sent them into the backyard to play. They ran out without arguing. "We all did a good job," Hannah said.

"Sure did." Roxie nodded and grinned.

Kathy filled a glass with cold water and drank it. "What do we do now?"

"Wait for Paula." Hannah sat at the table. "She can't say the house isn't clean this time."

"And we got most of the wax off the windows and filled the holes back in with the dirt clumps." Roxie looked very proud of herself.

Just then someone knocked at the back door. The girls exchanged startled looks, and then

Hannah ran to answer it. She opened the door and gasped in surprise to see Nell Wirt standing there. Hannah had told her their plans, but she hadn't expected Nell for another hour.

Nell rubbed her hands down her plaid dress and looked worried. "I had to come see if things were working like you thought."

"So far." Hannah smiled. "Come in and meet the others."

Nell shook her head. "I don't want to."

"Will you be back to watch the kids if Paula doesn't come on time?" That was the plan she and Nell had come up with, and Hannah wanted to make sure Nell still agreed to it.

Nell nodded and hurried away without looking back.

Hannah walked slowly to the kitchen. She hadn't found a chance to tell the Best Friends about Nell Wirt or her part in the plan. Why wouldn't Nell come inside and meet the others?

"Who was that?" Chelsea asked.

Before Hannah could answer Elise ran in, her face red. "Sam's choking on a sucker!"

With the Best Friends on her heels, Hannah raced out to the backyard. Sobbing, Rita stood beside Sam who was gagging and turning blue. Hannah picked Sam up and tipped him upside-down with his head almost on the ground and his heels in the air. She told Kathy to slap him firmly on the back. A sucker with a broken cardboard stick popped out of Sam's mouth onto the grass.

"I got a picture," Chelsea said proudly.

Hannah hugged Sam while he sobbed against her shoulder. His tears made her T-shirt wet.

"How'd you know what to do?" Kathy asked.

"I remember Mom did it once when Vivian was choking." Hannah carried Sam to the kitchen and sat down with him on her lap. Their faces white, Elise and Rita pressed close to her.

"You saved his life," Kathy said softly, smiling at Hannah.

Hannah trembled. "I never even stopped to think . . . I just acted."

"You did great." Roxie laughed and shook her head. "I froze. I mean, I turned to an ice cube."

"But not Hannah!" Kathy patted Hannah's shoulder.

"And I got it on film." Chelsea held up her camera as she smiled proudly at Hannah.

Hannah held Sam tighter. "I can't remember what Vivian choked on. But she was choking and couldn't breathe. So Mom held her upside-down and thumped her back." Hannah trembled. "I was scared."

Kathy sat across from Hannah. "Megan choked on a potato chip once, but we didn't have to do anything. She coughed it up, and Mom gave her a drink of water."

Chelsea set her camera on the table. "I'll take the film in today and get it developed. I wish we could show the whole world how you saved Sam's life."

"Like on TV." Roxie leaned on her elbows. "We could contact the TV station and see if they want to do a report about you, Hannah."

"You're a hero." Kathy pulled Rita onto her lap and held her.

Roxie motioned to Elise and had her share the chair. Roxie put her arm around Elise. "You're a hero too for coming to get us."

Elise leaned her head on Roxie. "We saw the sucker in the grass, but I didn't think Sam would pick it up. It was real yucky with grass and dirt on it and a broken stick. But he didn't care."

"It was mine," Rita said, her eyes wide. "I dropped it a long time ago."

Sam lifted his head and looked at Hannah. "I'm hungry."

Laughing, Hannah stood up and set Sam down on the chair. "I'll see what I can get you to eat." She found some graham crackers and gave some to Sam and the little girls.

Kathy looked at her watch. "I have to go in a few minutes. What if their mother doesn't come back in time?"

"I have it all taken care of." Hannah smiled. "I

told you I would. A woman I know is coming here and will take care of them."

"Who is it?" Roxie asked.

"Nell Wirt."

Roxie gasped and shook her head. "No! Not her, Hannah!"

"Why not?" Shivers ran down Hannah's spine as she waited for Roxie's answer.

"I can't tell you." Roxie motioned to the little girls and Sam. "It's too awful to say."

Hannah's head spun. She'd thought Nell Wirt was a fine woman who just happened to miss her old life and her farm. Was she wrong about Nell Wirt after all? "Then I don't know what to do."

"Call Grandma," Elise said.

Hannah looked at Elise in surprise. "Where is she?"

"Two houses away. Her name is Betty Slye."

Kathy looked up Betty Slye's phone number and called her. Kathy told her what was happening. "So, could you come watch the kids until Paula gets home?"

Hannah leaned forward while Kathy listened to the answer. Finally she hung up and slowly turned to the Best Friends. "What?" Hannah asked.

"She can't come. She's in the middle of making dinner."

"We can go over there," Elise said.

"We'll have to do something fast." Roxie tapped her watch. "Look how late it is."

Kathy looked out the window. "Paula's not out there."

"Call Mrs. Slye back and see if the kids can go over there," Chelsea said.

Kathy called back, but Mrs. Slye said it wasn't convenient to have the kids.

"She's mad at Mom," Elise said. "She gets mad a lot."

The girls exchanged looks. Hannah knew they were thinking just what she was—Paula's mom knew what she was like too.

Kathy looked out the window again. "What are we going to do?"

"Let Nell Wirt watch them." Hannah paced the kitchen and then stopped near the table. "Roxie, I've talked to her. She's nice. She's just a little strange, that's all."

Roxie rolled her eyes. "We'll talk about it later. But you'd better not have her."

Hannah looked helplessly at Chelsea and Kathy. They both shrugged. They hadn't even heard of Nell Wirt before now. "Who else can we call?"

Roxie spread her hands wide.

Kathy looked out the window again. "We have to do something! I say let Nell Wirt do it."

Roxie flung her arms out. "Oh, all right!" She

leaned close to Hannah and whispered, "I just hope you're not sorry."

Shivers trickled down Hannah's spine. She caught Roxie's arm and pulled her into the hallway. "What do you know about Nell Wirt?"

Roxie bit her lip. "She yelled at Faye, and she would've hit her if I hadn't stopped her."

"Oh, Roxie! Are you sure?"

"I saw her!" Roxie lowered her voice even more. "And she actually lives in a barn."

Hannah shook her head.

"My brother Eli told me so."

Chelsea poked her head out the kitchen door. "We have to hurry."

"I say let's have Nell Wirt take care of the kids." Hannah nudged Roxie. "Okay?"

Roxie wrinkled her nose. "I guess we have to. But how will we explain her to Paula Mercer?"

"We won't have to. Nell said she'd tell her she's doing Kathy a favor. Which she is." Hannah walked back into the kitchen. "We're going now. Kathy, I'll bring Nell in." Hannah hesitated. Would Nell suddenly start acting strange again and not come in?

While Kathy waited inside with the kids, Hannah hurried outdoors with Chelsea and Roxie. Hannah looked around the yard that was now clean and tidy. The lawn looked nice where they'd filled in the holes with the clumps of grass. "Nell? We're ready for you."

"How do you know she's even here?" Chelsea whispered as she looked around.

"She said she'd be here." Hannah swallowed hard. But would Nell really show up?

"She's really really strange," Roxie whispered as she darted a look around.

Just then Nell stepped out of the garage, tugging her purple hat low onto her gray head. "I'm here."

Hannah smiled as she introduced Nell to Roxie and Chelsea. "Chel wants to take your picture with the kids so we can prove you did watch them. Is that all right?"

Nell frowned, making the wrinkles in her face deepen. "I don't have on any lipstick."

"It's all right," Chelsea said as she lifted her camera. "Let's go inside. I'll take a picture, and then we have to leave."

With Roxie and Chelsea following, Hannah walked inside with Nell, who kept muttering she looked terrible without her lipstick. Kathy introduced Nell to the kids and told her about the baby's schedule. To Hannah's relief the kids weren't afraid of Nell at all. As Chelsea took the picture, Hannah looked smugly at Roxie. Roxie just shrugged.

Kathy jotted a note and tucked it under the edge of the kitchen phone. "Mrs. Wirt, the note tells who you are and that Paula is to pay you, and then you'll pay me."

"I'll make sure she gets it," Nell said grimly.

Before she left, Hannah pulled Nell aside and whispered, "Do you think you can manage the kids all right?"

Nell nodded. "I'm used to hard work."

"Let me know how it turns out. I'll be back from church before 9."

"I'll be in bed by then. I'll talk to you before you catch the school bus in the morning."

Hannah's eyes widened. "That's really early."

"I'm used to getting up early." Nell grinned. "I've been a farm woman all my life." She sobered. "Still would be if I had my say."

Hannah saw the sadness in Nell's eyes, and it made her feel sad too. She wanted to do something to make Nell happy again, but right now she couldn't think of anything. "See you in the morning."

Nell nodded.

Hannah hurried to her bike and pedaled toward home with the others. She glanced back. Was it safe to leave Nell Wirt with the Mercer kids? Maybe she should have asked her mom what she thought about all this, but it was too late for that now.

9

Taking Action

The next morning Hannah jumped in surprise, then whirled around to find Nell Wirt standing beside the rock in front of her house. The twins and Lena ran on to catch the bus. Hannah smiled and patted her racing heart. "You scared me. I guess I'm nervous or something. How'd it go last night?"

Nell tugged her gray sweater tightly around her. "Paula Mercer said she didn't owe me a dime. Nor Kathy either. She said Kathy didn't do the work she asked her to do."

"I can't believe it!" Hannah helplessly shook her head.

"She said the house was clean when she left, and she'd only asked Kathy to clean the kitchen cupboards."

"But that's not true!"

"I know."

"What'll we do now?"

"Take action!" Nell shook her fist in the air, and her eyes flashed with anger.

"But what can we do?"

"Something worthwhile, you can bet your boots!" Nell grinned, and her wrinkles deepened. "Run along now before you miss the bus."

"Thanks, Nell."

She smiled. "It's almost bearable to live here when I have something worthwhile to do."

Hannah chuckled. "Don't forget the mystery. We still have that to solve."

"Sure do." Nell squared her shoulders.

"See you after school."

Nell tipped her head. "Might not."

Hannah felt alarmed at the look on Nell's face. "Why?"

"Can't say." Muttering to herself, Nell hurried away.

Hannah ran for the bus, her sneakers slapping the sidewalk. What was Nell planning to do?

At the bus stop students of all sizes and ages waited for the bus. Their bright clothes made a colorful collage. A breeze fluttered the still-green leaves in the trees lining the sidewalk. At the edge of the noisy mass of boys and girls Hannah found Roxie and Chelsea. They were anxious to know Nell's news. Hannah told them but didn't say anything about Nell's strange behavior. Roxie mistrusted her enough as it was.

Chelsea held her books tightly to her chest. "We'll have to find a way to get the money from Paula Mercer. I mean it! This is terrible!"

"We'll all think of a plan, then talk after school." Roxie sighed. "I forgot—I can't right after school. But after dinner maybe."

"After dinner then." Hannah nodded just as the yellow-and-black bus braked to a noisy stop.

Someone pushed Hannah aside, and she lost her place in line. A muscle jumped in her cheek. She hated being knocked aside for anything. But that's the way it had always been and still was, and she couldn't do anything about it. Finally she stepped into the bus. Smells of cologne, sweat, and cigarette smoke clinging to clothes made her wrinkle her nose as she walked down the aisle.

Vivian caught her hand and tugged. "Sit with us."

Sherry looked up at Hannah. "Tell us what Nell Wirt said to you."

"Tell everything!" Lena bit her lip and widened her black eyes.

Hannah hesitated. She noticed the Best Friends didn't have room for her, so she dropped down beside the twins and Lena. It was an easy fit since the girls were so small.

The bus lurched and pulled away from The Ravines. Hannah settled back and told the girls how Nell had helped last night and that Paula

Mercer hadn't paid her or Kathy. "So we have to find a way to get her to pay."

"Tell Dad to make her," Sherry said.

Hannah shook her head. "She won't listen to Dad."

"Tell the F.B.I.," Vivian said.

Hannah listened to their suggestions the rest of the way to school. Most of them were impossible and some very funny.

Later at her locker Hannah took out her reading book as locker doors clanged up and down the hall. Students talked and laughed, and somebody played a few notes on a trombone. A girl at the next locker blew a bubble. It popped, and the smell of grape wafted out from it.

Just then Brianna Cobb stopped beside Hannah. Brianna looked ready to burst with excitement. "You'd love our first assignment in art!"

Hannah wanted to walk away, but she just couldn't. She wanted to know. "What is it?"

"A still-life of our choice! We can have up to five objects but must have at least three."

"What are you going to set up?" Hannah fell into step with Brianna as they walked around a group of boys and headed for reading class.

"I don't know for sure, but I think I'll do hair clips and barrettes and a mirror. Todd said he's going to do a cowboy hat, spurs, and a sheriff's star."

Hannah's hand itched to paint. She thought of all kinds of wonderful things she could set up. But of course she couldn't unless she did it on her own.

"We all paint the same still-life in class, but set our own up at home. That way Miss Norville said she could teach us the techniques."

Hannah's heart sank. Why even listen to Brianna go on and on? It hurt too much to hear about the class and know she couldn't join. "Talk to you later, Brianna." Hannah hurried into her homeroom before Brianna could say anything else.

The rest of the school day Hannah forced her thoughts off art and thought about ways to get the money from Paula Mercer. But she couldn't find an idea that would work.

At home Hannah looked for Nell near the rock, but she wasn't there. Inside Hannah changed into her old jeans and a pink T-shirt. She grabbed an apple and ran out the back door, biting into the apple as she went. Juice sprayed out from the crisp bite. The taste was tart, exactly the way she liked it. Across the street Gracie barked and Mike shouted happily. Tomorrow Mike had to return Gracie to Ezra Menski. Ezra and Roxie's grandma would be home from their honeymoon.

Hannah looked in the little red barn, but Nell wasn't there. Hannah ran across the Wirts' yard to the back porch. She tried the door, but it was locked. Gray mewed and scratched at the door. Frowning thoughtfully Hannah walked back across the yard. Where was Nell? Once again Hannah stopped at the little red barn. She pushed open the door. Nell's book lay on the chair. Under the book was a piece of lined paper. Hannah bit her lower lip. Should she look at the paper? Slowly she stepped into the barn. The warm air made the potting soil smell stronger.

Trembling, Hannah picked up the paper. Her name leaped out at her. It was a note from Nell Wirt! The handwriting was bold with large, looping letters. The note said, "I'm at Paula Mercer's place with some other folks. Come as soon as you can."

Hannah ran home to tell Mom where she was going and then grabbed her bike and pedaled fast toward Paula's house. Wind made Hannah's pink T-shirt billow out and forced her long hair to flap like crazy. At Paula's Hannah stopped abruptly, almost tumbling off her bike. Nell Wirt and a group of other people were walking up and down the sidewalk in front of Paula's house. Nell and the others carried signs and were chanting, "Paula Mercer doesn't pay what she owes! Paula Mercer is a cheat and a tightwad!"

Hannah's face burned, and she didn't know if she could—or should—join in. It was embarrassing to picket someone's house. She'd seen workers outside factories picket and heard them yell. On the news she'd seen them fight with each other. Would Paula come out and fight?

Nell spotted Hannah and waved to her. Nell wore her purple hat, black pants, and a purple-and-black blouse. Her cheeks were flushed pink, and today she wore bright red lipstick.

Hannah leaned her bike against a tree and ran around two women and a man to get to Nell. "Who are all these people?"

"Folks who never got paid . . . Or their kids worked for Paula and never got paid. They were all glad to do this."

"Does Paula know you're out here?"

"Of course. She came out once and yelled for us to leave, but I told her we wouldn't go until she paid us." Nell shook her head. "Adding everything together, Paula owes almost a thousand dollars! She's been doing this almost three years!"

"And nobody stopped her?"

"Nope." Nell giggled. "But that was before I came on the scene. Paula is wrong and must be stopped. Together we'll stop her!" Nell shook her sign that said, "PAULA MERCER OWES US MONEY!"

Hannah looked helplessly around. Three girls too young to be in school yet were carrying little signs and yelling.

Nell nudged Hannah. "I want you to ring the doorbell and demand your money while everyone watches."

Hannah trembled. "I don't think I can do that," she whispered.

"Sure you can! You have to!"

"I can't! Really."

"You can't give up." Nell looked very stern. "Never give up!"

Hannah backed away. She just couldn't let Paula yell at her in front of all those people! "I can't stay, Nell." With a low whimper Hannah ran to her bike and pedaled home.

In the garage she stood beside her bike rack with her head down and her shoulders slumped. Nell just didn't understand how it felt to be humiliated and hurt by others. Fighting back wasn't the answer. But did giving in do any good? Hannah groaned. She always gave in . . . and she probably always would.

Slowly Hannah walked outdoors into the bright sunlight. She leaned against the warm rock and looked across at Chelsea's house. Did Chelsea always give in? Hannah shook her head. Chelsea stood up for herself. "But she's not Ottawa," Hannah whispered hoarsely. "And neither is Nell Wirt. They don't know how it is."

Just then Chelsea ran out her door and across the street. Her long blue shirt flapped around her thin body. She waved a packet high over her head. "I got them! Wait'll you see!"

Hannah smiled at Chelsea's excitement.

"Look, Hannah!" Chelsea held out the packet. "It's the pictures from yesterday at Paula's house."

Hannah trembled as she took them. She looked through them quickly. They had turned out extremely well. "It's proof we did the work. But we didn't clean the kitchen cupboards, just like Paula said."

"She didn't tell Kathy to do that." Chelsea giggled. "But we did even more than she asked Kathy to do." Chelsea took the pictures and flipped through them until she found the one she wanted. "Look at this one where you're saving Sam's life."

Hannah studied it closely. She looked very tense as she held Sam upside-down. The sucker was midair between Sam's mouth and the ground. It was blurry, but she could tell it was a sucker. She shivered just thinking of the frightening situation, then handed the photo back to Chelsea.

"I'm going to put the photos on a poster and go show them to Paula Mercer right now. Kathy and Roxie are going too."

"I thought Roxie was doing something else."

"She got out of it. She said this is more important."

Hannah's insides quivered. Could she return to Paula's house with the Best Friends and join the picketing? She hesitated, then told Chelsea what Nell had done. "So there are a lot of people at Paula's place right now. I don't want to go back there."

"But this is our fight too!"

Hannah shook her head. "There are enough people already."

"We have to do our part."

"But it's so embarrassing!"

Chelsea lifted her chin, and her eyes flashed. "If we can stop Paula Mercer from cheating others, it'll be worth it."

Hannah wanted to sink out of sight. She knew she couldn't let the Best Friends down. She'd go with them to Paula's house. But it would be sooo hard!

10

Hannah's Decision

Hannah stood beside Chelsea and Roxie as Kathy rang Paula's doorbell. The picketers stood quietly on the sidewalk, their signs held high, their faces grim. The door opened immediately, and Paula stood there, looking angry.

"What do you want?"

"I came for my money from last night." Kathy didn't sound or look scared.

Hannah bit her lip. If she were Kathy, she'd faint on the spot.

"You didn't do the work I said to do. I don't owe you a dime!" Paula started to close the door, but Kathy stopped her.

Chelsea ran forward, the poster with the photos in her hand. "We can prove we did the work. It's all right here."

Paula's face turned as white as the clouds in the sky. "What's this?"

Chelsea stopped beside Kathy. "See? I took photos of what your place looked like, of us working, and what it looked like afterward."

Paula grabbed for the poster, but Chelsea leaped back with it.

"We want our money! We want our money!" the picketers chanted.

Hannah ducked behind a nearby tree. She didn't want Paula to see her and yell at her. Finally she heard the door slam. She peeked around. Paula was gone. Chelsea and Kathy were walking away from the front door laughing. They hadn't been embarrassed at all.

"Now can we go home?" Hannah asked as she stepped beside Roxie again.

"No way!" Roxie shook her head. "We should stay right here until she pays us."

"I can't," Hannah whispered, backing away. She waited until the Best Friends were talking with the picketers, then slipped quietly away. As she ran toward her bike, a car pulled up to the curb. A woman got out of the backseat.

"Hannah Shigwam?"

"Yes . . ." Hannah's body pricked with heat. Was the woman going to ask her about Paula and the picketers?

Suddenly the woman grabbed Hannah's arm, pushed her into the backseat, and slid in beside her.

Hannah cried out in fear, but she knew nobody

could hear her over the noise of the chanting. Silently she prayed for help and protection.

"Get out of here quick!" the woman snapped to the driver.

He nodded and pulled away with a roar. He drove around a corner so fast Hannah fell against the woman.

"Let me go! What're you doing with me?" Inside Hannah was *yelling* the words, but they came out a mere croak. She stared at the woman, who was looking straight ahead. She had a touch of gray in her brown hair and a determined look on her face. She wore dark blue pants and a lighter blue sweater. The driver was younger. His hair touched the collar of his red plaid shirt. He drove in silence for several minutes and finally pulled into a driveway and up into a garage. He looked over his shoulder at the woman.

"Need help getting her inside, Ma?"

"I can handle her. Want to come in for a cookie before you go on home?"

Hannah whimpered as the man shook his head. "Jeanette's waiting for me. I'll talk to you later."

"Thanks for helping." The woman dragged Hannah from the car and pushed her into the kitchen. "Sit down and stay there!"

Hannah collapsed onto a gray plastic-covered kitchen chair. The room was small and clean and smelled like coffee. The table and chairs filled most of the floor space. Sunlight shone through the window over the sink. "What do you want with me?" she asked hoarsely.

"I want you to stop them folks from harassing my daughter."

Hannah stiffened, and the hairs on the back of her neck stood on end. Was this woman really Betty Slye? "Paula Mercer is your daughter?"

"Yes, she is."

Hannah locked her icy hands in her lap. She was only two houses from Paula's house, but the driver had driven around so she wouldn't know that! Evidently Mrs. Slye didn't realize Hannah knew Paula lived only two houses away. It had been Kathy who'd talked on the phone to her last night. Hannah swallowed hard. "What can *I* do?"

"You're the one who got that old woman, Nell Wirt, nosing around about Paula. Now it's up to you to stop her."

"I can't stop her. She won't listen to me."

"She'd better." Betty Slye dropped to a chair and leaned on the formica-topped table. "You get her and all the others to stop, and I'll pay you what Paula owes you."

An idea popped into Hannah's head, but she made sure the excitement didn't show on her face or in her voice. She'd pretend to go along with Betty, then run away as soon as possible. And once she was away, she'd do everything she could to let the whole world know what Paula had done, no matter how embarrassing it was. "What about pay for the others?"

"You're joking, of course. I won't pay them anything! But I will pay you." Betty Slye narrowed her eyes. "I'll pay you double. Now, how can you pass up that deal?"

Hannah thoughtfully studied the woman. How could she pass it up? "Pay me first, then I'll talk to Nell."

"How do I know you'll keep your word?"

Hannah shrugged. "I guess you don't." Could she follow her wonderful idea? It would take a lot of courage to tell her story to whoever would listen.

"I'll pay you what Paula owes you, and when you call Nell Wirt and the others off, I'll pay you the rest."

"No! All of it now or I don't do it." Hannah trembled on the inside, but she didn't let it show. Silently she thanked God for giving her the strength to follow her plan.

Betty Slye jumped up and grabbed her purse. "Oh, all right!" She pulled out the money and dropped it on the table in front of Hannah. "Now that we have that settled, I'll take you home. It's a long drive."

Hannah bit back a sharp remark. She didn't dare reveal that she knew differently. She pushed the bills into her pocket. "I hope it doesn't take too long. My mom expects me to help make dinner."

"Paula used to help me make dinner." Betty Slye shook her head and sighed. "I don't know where that girl went wrong. She knows she should pay folks who work for her, but she gets a kick out of getting free labor." Her face hardened. "Let's get going. I want this mess cleared up now before somebody calls the police and gets my girl in deep trouble."

Hannah walked with Betty Slye to a small blue car in the garage. Betty fumbled with her keys, dropped them, and bent to pick them up. Hannah seized the opportunity and leaped away.

"Come back here!" Betty screamed.

Hannah ducked around the garage and behind a tall bush. She held her breath and waited. She saw Betty Slye run out of the garage and look up and down the street, then dash back into her garage. A minute later the angry woman roared out in her car and drove away fast. Hannah breathed a sigh of relief and raced down the sidewalk toward Paula's house. Suddenly she spotted Betty's little blue car, and her heart plunged to her feet. She ducked behind a tree and waited until the car drove past. Fear pricked her skin, and she silently prayed for courage. The car was a darker blue and a bigger car. It wasn't Betty's after all. Hannah giggled nervously.

She waited another minute and ran again.

Would the Best Friends and Nell still be at Paula's house? A shiver ran down Hannah's spine, and she slowed down. She saw that the crowd was still on the sidewalk, and she sighed in relief.

Just then she spotted Betty Slye's car parked across the street from Paula's house. Betty sat behind the steering wheel with her window down. She was looking all around.

Her heart pounding, Hannah dodged behind a row of bushes. She'd have to get to Paula's without Betty seeing her and trying to stop her.

She dodged from tree to tree and finally reached Paula's yard. For the first time she noticed a Channel 3 TV van. Her stomach tightened. Should she just keep going, or should she find a way to tell them her story? She shivered. Did she really want to take the chance that she'd be on TV for all the viewers to see? She shook her head. She couldn't do it. She just couldn't, no matter what she'd planned! She couldn't take a chance that she'd hear people say, "She's only an Indian—what does she know?"

She crept around a bush, out of sight of everyone. She peeked through the bush and watched the TV camera pan the area, then zoom in on Paula's front door. The Best Friends stood to one side, talking and looking concerned. She knew they wondered where she was. The camera pointed at Nell, and she quickly turned away and ducked her head. She wouldn't talk to the reporter. Hannah remembered seeing the woman many times on TV. She was tall and slender with blonde hair combed back off her face. She wore a light blue suit with a bold, bright red-and-purple scarf.

Hannah bit her lip. She had said she'd do something once she got away from Betty Slye. So why wasn't she? Was she a coward? God was with her—so why was she afraid? She closed her eyes and moaned, then remembered the Bible verse Dad had read at breakfast—Hebrews 13:6—"The Lord is my helper. I'll not fear what men shall do to me." Maybe that wasn't exactly what it said, but it was near enough. The Lord was her helper! She didn't have to fear or be embarrassed at what others would do to her.

"Thank You, Lord," she whispered. With God's help she would follow the plan she'd made at Betty Slye's house.

With her head high and her heart thundering, Hannah walked in sight of the crowd and right up to the TV reporter. "My name is Hannah Shigwam, and I have something important to say about Paula Mercer."

The reporter smiled, then quickly asked Hannah a few pertinent questions. When she was satisfied, she asked the cameraman to get ready. "Stand here beside me, Hannah. And don't let the camera scare you. Just talk to me as if we're carrying on a conversation with nobody else around."

"I'll try." Hannah glanced at the Best Friends. They waved at her and smiled proudly. She lifted her chin and got ready for the questions.

The reporter straightened her scarf and smiled into the camera. "This is Lisa Geha with more information about the strange happenings outside a residence in the small town of Middle Lake." She turned to Hannah. "I have a girl with me who worked for Paula Mercer and got this whole thing started. Tell us your name please."

Hannah's mouth turned bone-dry. Could she even speak? Then a peace settled over her, and she smiled. She knew the Best Friends were praying for her. "I'm Hannah Shigwam, and I live at The Ravines." She told about being a *King's Kid* and about being hired to clean the playroom in Paula's house. She told everything she remembered, and even about sending Kathy there and having Chelsea take pictures. "The girls I'm talking about are over there. Chelsea has the photos with her—photos that prove we did the work we were supposed to do."

Lisa Geha waved the girls over while the cameraman turned the video camera on them. Lisa had the girls introduce themselves, then held up the photos as they talked. She especially liked the story of Hannah saving Sam from choking. Finally Lisa asked Hannah if there was anything else she wanted to say.

Hannah told about being picked up by Betty Slye, Paula's mom, and what had happened.

Hannah held up the money. "Here's the money she paid me to get everyone to stop picketing and to leave." Hannah heard the others gasp, but she couldn't look at them. Her legs were beginning to wobble, and she gripped Kathy's hand for support and held on tight.

After what seemed like forever, the Channel 3 crew drove away.

"We're going to be on TV tonight!" Chelsea giggled and nudged Roxie.

"We're famous!" Roxie tugged on Hannah's arm. "I'm glad you talked to Lisa Geha. That took a lot of courage."

"I did it because I knew Jesus was with me and was helping me."

"I'm going to be sure and tape the news tonight," Kathy said with a laugh. "That way we can watch as often as we want."

"I need to find Nell and talk to her." Hannah looked around, but she couldn't see Nell anywhere in the crowd of people. "Do you girls see her?"

None of them did. "She's so strange—she probably just wandered away," Roxie said.

Hannah didn't think so, but she didn't say anything. "I have to get home."

"Me too," they all three said, then giggled.

Later Hannah left her bike in the garage and ran to the little red barn. She looked inside, but Nell wasn't there. Hannah glanced at the house. Tom and

Julie Wirt would be home from work soon. Maybe Nell was making dinner.

Shrugging, Hannah ran to her house and slipped inside. "Mom, wait'll you hear what happened," she called.

Later the family gathered around the TV, talking excitedly. Hannah's heart hammered so hard against her rib cage she thought nobody could hear the TV over it. She held her breath as Lisa Geha introduced her, then let her talk. They'd cut her story down a lot.

Suddenly Paula Mercer was on the TV screen. Hannah sat bolt upright. She didn't know Paula had been interviewed.

"I want everyone to know that the group called the *King's Kids* is a rip-off! They say they'll do the work, but they don't. They cheat! And they stole from me—twenty dollars and a bottle of expensive perfume. Friends of mine have said the same thing. The kids even waxed my windows and dug up my front yard. They pretended to save my little boy's life, but they staged the whole thing and took pictures of it. It's sad to think those kids call themselves *King's Kids* considering that the King they're supposedly representing is Jesus. They're making a mockery of Jesus, and I don't like that at all!"

"Did you hear her?" Hannah cradled herself with her arms and rocked back and forth. Would anyone believe the terrible lies?

11

Trouble for the King's Kids

Just after the newscast ended the phone rang, and Hannah almost jumped out of her skin. Dad answered it in the kitchen, then called her.

"It's Chelsea." He hugged Hannah. "Tell her we know Paula told lies on the news broadcast."

"Thanks, Dad." Hannah leaned against the kitchen counter and said, "Hi, Chel."

"Isn't it just awful!"

"For sure! What'll we do now?" Hannah sank to the floor with her back against the counter. She shouldn't have told her story to anyone, especially not to the TV news reporter!

"Dad said he thinks Channel 3 will get a flood of calls from folks who were happy with the *King's Kids'* work. He called them just before I called you. Mom said we could send around a petition stating that the *King's Kids* are good, hard workers and worth their pay. After we get a lot of people to sign it, we can send it to Lisa Geha, and maybe she'd report it on the news."

Hannah bit her lip. She wanted to give up on the whole business. She talked a while longer and hung up. Immediately the phone rang. She answered it.

"Hannah Shigwam?"

"Yes . . ." It was a woman's voice she didn't recognize.

"You should be ashamed of yourself for telling all those lies on TV. It's like I always say—you can't trust the word of an Indian!"

Hannah slammed the receiver down and covered her face with trembling hands.

"What's wrong?" Mom pulled Hannah close to her heart and held her tightly.

Between sobs Hannah repeated what the woman had said. "Maybe everybody thinks that!"

The phone rang again, and Mom answered it.

Hannah waited beside her, ready to spring away if it was bad. Mom smiled, and Hannah relaxed.

Mom hung up and turned to Hannah. "That was Ezra Menski. He and Emma are back now. He saw the news, and he wants you to know he'll do everything he can to help."

The phone rang again, and again Hannah

jumped. She stood back as Mom answered. The doorbell rang, and Hannah jumped again.

"I'll get the door," Dad called. The twins and Lena ran after him.

Hannah chewed on her bottom lip as she waited to see who was on the phone and who was at the front door.

Mom held her hand over the receiver. "It's Tom Wirt. He wants to know if you saw his grandma."

Hannah nodded. "She was at Paula Mercer's, but she left before I did. I didn't see her after that."

Mom told Tom Wirt what Hannah had said, then hung up with a worried frown. "He says he'll drive over to the Mercer house in case she went back to picket again. He's worried because of her health."

Hannah tensed. "She seemed all right to me."

Mom shrugged. "Well, Tom is concerned." Mom frowned. "I've never even seen his grandma. Is she shy?"

Strange was more like it, but Hannah didn't say that. "She's sad because she can't live on her farm."

Dad walked into the kitchen with the twins and Lena following him. "Jake from next door was at the door. He tried to call, but the line was busy. He wanted us to know he believes you, Hannah."

She sighed in relief.

"And if he does, many others do too." Dad rubbed his hand over Hannah's shoulder. "Most important, we know the truth—and, even better,

God knows the truth. Walk with your head high, Hannah."

"Like this." Lena lifted her chin and squared her shoulders, then walked across the kitchen.

The twins giggled and copied her.

Hannah couldn't even smile. While Mom and Dad talked, Hannah slipped out the back door and stood in the yard. It was still light out, but the warmth of the sun was gone. She glanced toward the Wirts' yard. Had Tom found Nell? Would he even know to look in the barn?

Hannah walked between the bushes and into the soft grass. The barn door was open, but the shadows were too deep to see inside this far away. Hannah walked closer until she stood at the door. "Nell?"

"Who asked you here?"

"Tom is worried about you."

"Then he should let me go home where I belong!" Nell tugged Hannah inside. "I don't want him seeing you out here. It might make him think to look in here." She laughed dryly. "He never thinks to look here. What woman in her right mind would sit in this little building? But it's a barn, and I like it." Nell sank down in her chair and folded her hands in her lap. "Well? Why are you here?"

"I was looking for you."

"You found me."

Hannah sank cross-legged to the floor. "Did you see the news?"

"Is there a TV in here?"

Hannah laughed. "I guess not."

"So, were you on the news?"

"Yes." Hannah told Nell about the broadcast and the bad phone call. "I wish I'd kept my mouth shut!"

"You give up too soon, Hannah Shigwam— you know that?" Nell shook her bony finger at Hannah. "You got God on your side! You think He'd give up? No! And neither should you."

Hannah laced her fingers together. She knew what Nell was saying was true.

"You're important to God, Hannah. Never forget that! He loves you, and He wants you to love Him."

"I do," Hannah whispered.

"Then trust Him to help you all the time, not just part of the time. He says you're more than a conqueror. You have to believe it and act like it. How can you if you give up so easily?"

Hannah swallowed hard. "But it hurts too much to have people say bad things to me because I'm Ottawa."

"You can choose to be hurt or choose to let it run off you like water off a duck's back." Nell tapped Hannah's shoulder. "You ever see water on a duck? Its feathers are waterproof, and rain or

water run right off. That's how God made ducks."
Nell grinned. "God made you with a free will—the
will to chose how you feel and how you act and
what you do. He gave you the strength to be an
overcomer. But you have to choose to accept His
strength and use it." Nell chuckled. "I sound like a
preacher, don't I? But what I'm saying is true."

Hannah brushed a tear from her lash. "How do
I quit giving up?"

"Make the decision to." Nell leaned forward.
"It's up to you, Hannah. It's as easy as that."

"It doesn't seem easy."

"You have the God of this entire universe helping you!" Nell spread her arms wide and almost hit
the handle of the lawn mower.

"You're right," Hannah whispered. Looking at
it that way, it was easy to keep going instead of giving up. But could she when it came right down to it?

"Of course I'm right! I always am."

With a laugh Hannah stood. "I'd better get
home. And you should get to the house. Your grandson is worried about you."

Sighing heavily, Nell pushed herself up. "I gave
up, and I lost my farm. Don't let that happen to you,
Hannah. Don't give up and lose something you
love."

Hannah thought of the Tuesday art class and
all the other things she'd wanted to do but hadn't
because of being turned away. If she hadn't given up,

she'd be in the art class. She might even be able to join the Photography Club and play on the tennis team.

Nell patted Hannah's arm. "We'll find a way to clear the *King's Kids*—you'll see."

"Thanks." Hannah smiled. "And what about the mystery? So much has been going on, we didn't solve that yet."

"But we will! *Somebody* waxed the windows and dug holes in the yard. Since somebody did it, somebody else can solve it. And we're that somebody!"

Hannah laughed. "We sure are!" She started out the door, then looked over her shoulder. "I'll walk you to the house."

Nell sighed. "Sure . . . All right . . . I can't stay out here all night long, can I?"

"No. The barn is too small, and the nights get too cold." Hannah fell into step with Nell and walked to the back porch. Gray meowed.

"It's not right for Gray to stay on a leash. An animal was meant to roam free."

"But he'd get run over if he did."

"I guess you're right about that." Nell slowly opened the door and stepped into the closed-in porch. Gray rubbed against her ankle, and she bent down to stroke him. "Good night, Hannah."

"Good night . . . And thanks." Hannah smiled.

How could anyone think Nell was a witch? She was kind and gave good advice.

Hannah ran across to her house and slipped through the door. She heard the others in the kitchen. It still smelled like fried chicken as she walked in. Mom and the girls sat at the table.

"There you are!" Mom motioned to a chair. "We're having hot cocoa. Want a cup?"

"Sure." Hannah filled a cup, dropped in a marshmallow, and sat down. "Where's Dad?"

"Burke cried, and he ran up to check on him."

"You're famous, Hannah." Lena sighed. "I wish *I* was!"

Vivian nudged Sherry. "We're going to sell your autograph in school tomorrow. We'll be rich!"

Hannah laughed. "I don't think so, girls."

Mom finished her cocoa and then picked up Dad's cup and sipped from it. She set the cup down. "Kathy and Roxie both called while you were outdoors. And Chelsea called again. I said you'd call them back. They said you might not be able to get through. Their phones have been ringing off the hook too."

Hannah looked over at their phone. "It's not ringing."

Mom laughed. "Dad shut it off. I told your friends he was going to, so they said they wouldn't try to get you."

Hannah drank the last of her cocoa, enjoying the rich chocolate and the gooey marshmallow.

"They might've shut off their phones by now too." Mom shook her head. "I can't believe so many people called."

"Were they good or bad calls?"

"Only about three bad ones, and the rest were all good."

"I'm glad!" Hannah put her cup in the dishwasher and hurried to the study. She called Chelsea first since she had a phone right in her own room. She didn't have her own number, but she said she wanted to get one as soon as she could afford it. Her line was busy. So were Roxie's and Kathy's.

Hannah ran to the kitchen. "Mom, could I go to Chelsea's to talk to her?"

"Sure. But be back before 9."

Hannah grabbed a light jacket and hurried out the door. Just as she started down her walk she saw Chelsea and Roxie coming across the street. They all three met at the big rock and laughed because they'd thought to meet at the same time.

"Too bad Kathy's not here," Hannah said.

Just then a car stopped in the street, and Kathy jumped out and ran to join them. The girls laughed and greeted her excitedly.

"My mom is going to visit your mom, Chel, so she said I could come too."

Hannah led the way to the backyard, where

they all sat on the deck. Lights glowed from the windows of houses all around. A dog barked in the distance. The smell of coffee drifted out from a house nearby.

"So shall I call this meeting to order?" Chelsea asked as she zipped up her jacket.

Hannah laughed. "Is it a *King's Kids* meeting or a Best Friends Club meeting?"

"Both." Chelsea grinned. "Might as well be."

"We haven't found out who waxed Paula's windows or dug up her yard." Hannah pushed back her hair and frowned. "I think once we do that we'll be able to deal better with Paula. She really thinks we—or should I say I?—did it."

"A lot of people had motive and opportunity," Kathy said. "But out of all of them, who would actually do it?"

"None of us—and none of the other *King's Kids* either." Roxie wrapped her arms around her knees and looked very serious. "And I can't imagine any of the people picketing the house today would do it. What do you girls think?"

Chelsea shook her head. "None I talked to."

"How about Paula's own mother? She might do something that drastic." Kathy nudged Hannah. "She kidnapped you."

Hannah nodded. "Tomorrow we'll talk to her and see. We could see if she has a little shovel. Nell said paraffin wax is a common household item. We have a wax crayon that we used when we decorated Easter eggs."

"We have wax to use on our toboggan," Roxie said.

"I've never been on a toboggan," Chelsea said.

"You will be this winter!" Hannah laughed. "We'll take you to the steep hill right outside of town where everybody goes. You'll ride like the wind."

Roxie nodded with a grin. "Snow in your face, and maybe a wipeout and you'll get buried in a drift. You'll like tobogganing."

They talked about winter for a while, and then Chelsea said, "I want each one of us to take a petition around tomorrow after school and get as many signatures as possible. The petition will say: 'I know the boys and girls in *King's Kids* are reliable, trustworthy people. They're hard workers and very honest.' We'll send copies to Channel 3, and we'll also have copies to use in case someone new wants to employ us, but isn't quite sure they can trust us."

"Good thinking. There's only five dollars in the treasury. I hope that'll cover the cost."

"What about the money Betty Slye gave you today?" Kathy asked.

Hannah reached in her pocket and pulled it out. "I forgot all about it! Sure . . . it's more than enough to cover the cost of copies and postage. But

I think we should divide this among us to pay for doing the work at Paula's."

"I say let's put it away until this whole issue is resolved." Kathy shrugged. "I think it would be the smartest thing to do."

Hannah nodded. "I was thinking I might even return it to Betty Slye."

"What?" the others cried together.

"*She* doesn't owe it to us. Paula does."

Chelsea sighed. "You're right. Let's vote on it."

Hannah lifted her hand. "I vote we keep it until everything is settled, then return it."

Chelsea raised her hand. "Me too. Roxie? Kathy?"

They both agreed.

"I've been thinking about that wax on the windows at Paula's house," Roxie said.

Hannah leaned forward with interest.

"It seemed more like white crayon instead of toboggan wax. Don't you think, Chel?"

She frowned thoughtfully and finally nodded. "Yeah . . . It *was* white crayon!"

"And the marks were at the very bottoms of the windows." Hannah's mind whirled. "The holes in the yard were shallow. Maybe a little kid did it! Maybe Elise!"

"It's sure possible." Chelsea nodded slowly. "We'll check into it tomorrow."

"We have a lot to do tomorrow," Hannah said. "Maybe we should all skip school."

"Oh, sure—I can see our parents letting us do that." Kathy giggled. "We'll just have to get more help—from other *King's Kids.*"

"Great idea!" Chelsea jumped up. "That's just what we'll do! I'll call several of them tonight and set it up for right after school."

Hannah stood with the others. "See you all tomorrow."

"Hey, what's our Scripture?" Roxie asked.

Hannah smiled. "I have one. Hebrew 13:6. 'The Lord is my helper. I'll not fear what men shall do to me.'" She lifted her chin. She would never forget the wonderful promise as long as she lived.

12

The Guilty One

Hannah looked down the sidewalk at the mass of students waiting for the bus at the end of The Ravines. They were chanting *her* name! She almost turned and ran back home, but she remembered God was with her and she didn't have to fear what the kids would do to her. She lifted her chin and kept walking.

Laughing, Lena ran back and caught Hannah's hand. "You're famous! I bet the twins will make a fortune selling your autograph."

A redheaded girl stepped away from the crowd and shouted, "Hey, Shigwam, save any more lives? Dig up any more yards?"

Hannah's face burned with embarrassment. But then she remembered when she sat in the little barn with Nell and she again heard Nell say, "You choose to be hurt or embarrassed or you let it roll off you like water off a duck's back." Hannah sucked in air. She'd choose to let it roll right off her! Without a word she walked up to Roxie and Chelsea, who stood with several *King's Kids*.

Chelsea patted Hannah's arm. "Don't even pay attention to that girl."

"I won't!" And Hannah wouldn't. She refused to think about it or get angry at the girl.

Rob McCrea smiled at Hannah. "We're going to see that everybody believes you and knows the *King's Kids* aren't cheaters."

The words warmed Hannah, and she smiled.

Other *King's Kids* encouraged Hannah too. Kids who didn't work for *King's Kids* also told Hannah they believed her and that they hadn't believed Paula Mercer at all. Some of the kids had been cheated by Paula themselves, and they told Hannah so. More kids talked to her before the bus arrived than ever before. They didn't seem to notice or care that she was Ottawa.

Later at her locker in school Brianna Cobb ran up to Hannah. "I saw you on TV last night! You told your story like you weren't nervous at all!"

Hannah chuckled. "I was nervous, but I had to tell what had happened."

"Well, you did a great job! I wish I could've been there."

"It was scary." Hannah unfolded the petition Chelsea had given her. She explained to Brianna what it was. "Will you sign it?"

"Of course!" Brianna quickly signed it, then held her books tightly to her and looked closely at Hannah. "I signed that—now how about you signing up for art class? There's still room for you."

Hannah stiffened. Here it was! Could she do it? She remembered God's promise, and she smiled. "I'm ready!"

"Good. I'll go with you."

"Thanks." Hannah hurried to the office with Brianna beside her. Several students called out to Hannah, and she answered them or just waved. In the office she walked up to the desk. Jane, one of the women who had been there before, was working there. Hannah's knees wobbled, but she refused to pay attention to them. "I'd like to sign up for the Tuesday art class with Miss Norville."

Jane looked through her papers. "It's not here. It must be full."

Hannah looked at Brianna, and she nodded. Hannah turned back to the woman. "Could you look again? I know there's still room for me."

Jane scowled but looked again. "Sorry. The paper isn't here."

Hannah's heart plunged to her feet. If only she'd listened to Brianna and tried again sooner! Now she'd lost out on the art class just like Nell had lost her farm!

Brianna nudged Hannah. "There *is* room," she whispered softly.

Taking a deep breath Hannah said, "Call Miss Norville and ask her please."

"That's not necessary."

Hannah trembled, but Brianna was right, and she wouldn't back down. Not this time! "There *is* room, and I *do* want to sign up."

Jane grabbed up the phone and jabbed the three numbers to Miss Norville's room. "Your art class on Tuesday is full, isn't it?"

Hannah's heart thundered, but she didn't run away.

The woman slowly hung up the receiver. "I don't know where the sheet is, but you can sign up. I'll make out a new sheet, and when I find the old one I'll add you to it."

"Thank you!" Hannah signed her name, then turned to Brianna and giggled happily. They hurried out of the office toward their homeroom.

Suddenly a boy jerked on Hannah's hair. She cried out and pried his fingers loose.

"Cut that out!"

He pushed his face almost into hers. "Paula Mercer is my cousin, and I know she wouldn't do the things you said she did! You're a liar, and I'm going to make sure everybody knows it!"

Hannah's blood turned to ice. How she wanted to disappear in a puff of smoke, but she stood her ground. She would not be hurt by what the boy said. *She* knew the truth about herself and about Paula.

"I told the truth. If she is your cousin, you know I told the truth!"

The boy pushed her hard, but Brianna kept her from falling. He ran off down the hall. Hannah swallowed hard and tried to stop shaking.

"Don't let Joe bother you," Brianna said.

"I won't," Hannah whispered. And she meant it!

After school, on her way to get on the bus, Hannah was mobbed again, but she was able to get two pages of names on her petition.

At home Mom said, "Hannah, Nell Wirt called this morning and said she left a note for you. She said you'd know where."

Hannah nodded. Nell meant the barn. "I'll be right back, Mom."

Hannah ran to the barn. She opened the door, and heat rushed out along with the smell of potting soil. She found the note on the chair. She read it, then read it again aloud as if she couldn't believe what she was reading. "Good-bye, my Indian friend. I'm going back to my farm. I gave up too soon! As for the mystery—you won't have any trouble solving it. You have friends who'll gladly help you. I'll miss you. Nell."

Hannah bit her lip. How could Nell go back to her farm? It had been sold to someone else.

Slowly Hannah walked out of the barn and closed the door. She saw Gray running across the grass without a leash. Nell had probably wanted Gray to be free too.

"Here, Gray! Here, kitty!" Hannah bent down with her hand out and called Gray again. He meowed and finally ran to her. She picked him up. He was soft and smelled dusty. She carried him to the porch and put him inside. "I'd like you to be free too, Gray, but I don't want you getting run over by a car."

Sighing, Hannah walked home, Nell's note in her hand. Had Nell left a note for Tom and Julie? Or would they come home from work, not know where she was, and be worried about her again?

Deep in thought Hannah walked into the house. She'd tell Mom about Nell and ask her to help her decide what to do. But Mom was busy with baby Burke. The phone rang, and Hannah answered it. It was Paula Mercer! Hannah almost dropped the phone.

"Hannah, I can't take it anymore . . . the picketing . . . the phone calls . . . Come over here and I'll give you your money and the money for everyone else."

Hannah's heart leaped. "I'll be right there."

"Come yourself or you won't get a dime!"

Hannah started to speak, but Paula hung up. Hannah tapped her finger to her lip. No way would she go alone to Paula's house! Hannah phoned the Best Friends and told them about the conversation.

"Let's call all the *King's Kids* and all go at the same time."

"Good idea," Chelsea said.

Several minutes later Hannah rode her bike toward Paula's house. Several *King's Kids* and the Best Friends were beside and behind her. Many kids who weren't *King's Kids* joined them as they rode down the street. As each new one arrived, someone explained their plan. They all knew to stay out of sight while Hannah rang the doorbell, then swarm the place if Paula tried anything funny.

Hannah stopped on the sidewalk at Paula's house. The picketers were gone. She'd expected them to still be there. She left her bike on the lawn and slowly walked to the door. She wanted to look over her shoulder to make sure everyone was there, but she didn't. They were all so quiet, she wondered if they'd left. "They wouldn't," she muttered.

Taking a deep, steadying breath, Hannah rang the doorbell. She heard the melody of it inside the house. She peeked over her shoulder. No one was in sight, but she was sure she heard whispers. A warm wind rustled the leaves of the trees. The smell of a freshly cut lawn drifted over from across the street.

Suddenly the door opened, and Elise stood there, a sucker in her mouth. She pulled it out with a loud *pop*. "Mom said to come in."

Hannah caught Elise's hand and tugged her out. "Are you mad at me?"

Elise shook her head. "No . . . But Mom is."

Hannah bent down and looked eye to eye with Elise. "I think I know who used a white crayon and drew across the windows."

Elise gasped. "It wasn't me!"

"And I think I know who used a little play shovel from the sandbox and dug holes in the yard."

Elise shook her head hard. "It wasn't me!"

Hannah smoothed back Elise's brown hair. "You must've been really angry at your mom to do those things."

Elise's chin quivered. "She said I was ugly."

"But you're not ugly." Hannah wiped a tear off Elise's cheek. "All you have to do is look in the mirror and see how pretty you are."

"I had on my new blue dress, and she said I was ugly and my dress was ugly."

"I'm sorry. You showed me your dress. It's very pretty."

Elise looked at the windows. "So I drew on the windows and dug up the grass so they'd be ugly."

"Does your mom know you did it?"

Elise shook her head. "You won't tell her, will you?"

Hannah smiled. "No. But I think you should."

"No way!"

"I'll help you."

Elise thought for a while. "I don't know . . . I might tell her."

Hannah kissed Elise's cheek. "Go tell your mom I'm here to get my money."

"She's upstairs with the baby. She said go on up."

Hannah narrowed her eyes thoughtfully. She wasn't going to fall into another trap. "Elise, run up and tell her I'm coming. I'll be right up."

"Okay." Elise dashed away, leaving the door open.

Hannah turned and motioned, then put her finger to her lips for silence.

Chelsea, Roxie, and Kathy led the way, and they all ran quietly to Hannah.

"I'm going upstairs to see Paula. All of you come inside and sit down. If I need you, I'll shout." Butterflies fluttered in Hannah's stomach, but she managed to smile.

She held the door wide until everyone was inside. She counted twenty kids. They swarmed into the living room and sat on the floor.

"Hannah!"

She looked out the door. Ezra Menski was hurrying toward her, his cane in his hand. He had a dark tan from being in Hawaii. His pants and shirt hung loose on his tall, bony frame. She laughed in delight. "Ezra! I'm so glad to see you!"

He hugged her, and she smelled mint on his breath. "I saw all of you heading this way, so I followed in my car."

"The others are waiting inside. Chelsea will tell you the plan."

Leaning on his cane, Ezra walked into the living room.

Smiling, Hannah closed the door and ran lightly upstairs to the nursery. She heard Elise, Rita, and Sam in the playroom. Hannah stood in the nursery doorway. She smelled baby powder. Paula was just laying the baby in his crib. She turned and glared at Hannah. Hannah wanted to run away, but she didn't.

Paula motioned for Hannah to step out into the hallway, and then Paula closed the nursery door. "You've caused me a lot of trouble, Hannah Shigwam!"

Hannah led Paula partway down the stairs so the others could hear everything she said. Paula hurried along beside her, going on and on about the hardship she'd been through the last few days with the noisy picketers. Hannah stopped so Ezra and the kids in the living room could hear without Paula seeing them.

"You said to come get the money you owed me," Hannah said loudly enough so everyone could hear. Paula was already talking loudly enough for the entire neighborhood to hear.

"I will never *never* pay you or the others!" Paula's face turned beet-red, and she doubled her fists.

"Then why'd you tell me to come over?"

Flipping back her long hair, Paula laughed wickedly. "So I could say you stole my husband's new watch. Elise smashed it with a hammer because she got angry. I threw it away, but nobody knows that—not even Sean. And he'll never know it! I'll tell him you stopped in today for your money, but I didn't have it, so you took his watch. It's worth about five hundred dollars. You'll be in *big* trouble this time."

Hannah shook her head. "Nobody will believe I stole the watch."

"Oh, but they will! It'll be your word against mine."

"No . . . No, it won't. We have all kinds of witnesses." Hannah grinned. "Look in your living room."

Paula leaped into the living room, then screamed in outrage. She turned back to Hannah. "It's only a bunch of kids! Who'll believe kids over me?"

"A lot of adults," Ezra said as he stepped forward.

Paula gasped and clamped her hands to her red cheeks. "Ezra!"

"It's me all right. You know folks will believe me."

Hannah watched the color drain from Paula's face.

140

Ezra patted Paula's shoulder. "Give it up, Paula. I can remember how embarrassed you used to get when your grandpa tried conning folks. You don't want to be known for that like he was, do you?"

Paula trembled. She shook her finger at Hannah. "She started it, Ezra. She came over here and waxed my windows and dug up my yard."

"No, she didn't, Mom." Elise stood on the stairs looking down at her mother.

Paula frowned up at Elise. "How do you know?"

Elise burst into tears. "I did it when I was mad at you!" She ran down and pressed her face against Hannah.

Hannah held Elise and looked at Paula. "You probably knew she did it, just like you knew she smashed your husband's watch."

Paula shivered.

"Is that right, Paula?" Ezra asked in a gentle voice.

Paula looked down at the carpet, then finally nodded.

"Pay Hannah and the others what you owe them, Paula. You know you want to, but it's all gotten out of hand." Ezra caught Paula's hand and held it. "Think back to the little girl who came to me in tears because of her grandpa. Do you want your kids in tears over your actions?"

"No," Paula whispered. She pulled free and brushed at her eyes. "I'll get my purse." She ran upstairs.

Hannah lifted Elise's face. "Your mom is really sorry for what she did, but she doesn't know how to say it. Please, Elise, don't do mean things when you get angry. Instead, talk to your mom and tell her how you feel."

Elise nodded. "I'll try."

Paula ran down the stairs with some cash and her checkbook in her hand. She counted out what she owed Hannah, then looked at the others. "Tell me what you have coming to you, and I'll write you checks for everything I owe you."

Hannah stepped close to Ezra and whispered, "Thanks." She'd thank the others on the way home. Maybe she'd even invite them all over for ice cream. They just might come even though she was Ottawa!

13

Art Class and Everything Else

Sunday afternoon Hannah carried ice cream cones to ten kids sitting on her deck. Yesterday she'd had a bunch of kids over to play games and have ice cream, but today they were only having ice cream. Mom and Dad didn't want them there all afternoon because they were too noisy. Dad liked his Sunday afternoons to be quiet, so he could take a nap if he felt like it.

"Is there any news about Nell Wirt?" Chelsea asked as she sat down on an empty bench.

Hannah sat beside her, and they both licked their ice cream. Hannah had chocolate and Chelsea vanilla. "Tom said he found her at the farm. She agreed to return with him Monday, but she wants to spend the weekend at a motel near the farm."

"I wish we knew someone with a farm near

Middle Lake —someone who'd like to have Nell live with them."

"Chel, that's a great idea!" Hannah jumped up. "Hey, everybody! Listen to me!" When they were quiet she said, "Who knows anyone living on a farm near here? Nell Wirt wants to live on a farm, and we want to find a farm for her. Will you all help look for one?"

"Sure," several kids said.

They talked about finding Nell a farm, then switched the conversation to school. Finally Hannah had to tell them it was time to leave. The Best Friends stayed behind to help clean up. When they finished they all sat on the deck to talk.

Hannah turned to Roxie. "Is it too late for me to sign up for tennis?"

"I don't think so. I thought you didn't like tennis."

"I do. It's just that I never got to play before." Hannah didn't tell them that she'd been turned away. This time she wouldn't let that happen.

"Do you know how?"

"Sure."

"Maybe the four of us could play at the park sometime." Kathy's eyes sparkled with excitement. "Chel, do you play tennis?"

Chelsea nodded. "I would've joined the group, but I didn't really have time to do that and photography."

Hannah leaned forward. "When's the contest deadline?"

"Next week."

Hannah smiled. "I might join the Photography Club. I wanted to last year."

"Do it then!" Chelsea squeezed Hannah's arm. "We'd have fun together."

Hannah thought of all the things she'd always wanted to do but hadn't done because of being pushed away. Now she could do everything! She looked at Kathy. Well, maybe she couldn't be a cheerleader—not this year anyway.

On Monday Hannah hurried to the photography classroom and signed up for the club. She stuck the details for the contest in her notebook and hurried to her homeroom. She'd sign up for tennis during P.E. Excitement bubbled up inside her, and it was hard to pay attention in class.

After school, at home, Hannah changed into shorts and a pink T-shirt. She was going to the park to practice tennis. She'd asked Roxie to go with her, but she couldn't. So she asked Brianna Cobb, and she'd quickly agreed. They were to meet at the park.

Hannah poked her head into the kitchen where Mom was having a snack with the twins and Lena. "I'm going now, Mom."

"Did you go see Nell?"

"Is she home again?"

Mom frowned. "Hannah, I told you when you

first came in that Nell was back and wanted to see you right after school."

Hannah sighed heavily. "I guess I could see her for a couple of minutes." She started to leave, then came back. "Mom, may I use your tennis racket?"

"As long as you're careful."

"Thanks!"

"Do you have homework, Hannah?"

"A little."

"Give yourself plenty of time to finish it."

"Sure . . . Okay." Hannah hurried to the closet, got the racket, and ran outdoors and around back. She hurried to the little red barn and looked in. Nell wasn't there. Hannah shook her head and looked at her watch. She'd see Nell later.

At the park Hannah found Brianna waiting on a bench outside the fenced-in tennis courts. Three courts were being used, and one was still empty. The girls hurried over to it.

"I'm not very good," Brianna said as she bounced the green ball.

"Neither am I. But we can have fun." Hannah ran to her side of the court. She felt lighter than air. She, Hannah Shigwam, was playing tennis!

Brianna served, but the ball hit the net. It took three tries for her to get it over. Hannah hit it back but not hard enough to get it over the net. They giggled and shook their heads. Hannah was glad Roxie hadn't been able to play with her. Roxie was really good at tennis. After an hour the girls decided to quit. They walked off the court and sat on the bench in the shade.

Hannah wiped sweat from her face. "I don't know if I'll ever be any good at tennis."

"My sister Tory is on the high school team, and she practices hours and hours. She started playing in fifth grade and has been playing ever since."

"Hours of practice?" Hannah wrinkled her nose. How could she practice that much?

"And in the winter she has to pay to play in an inside court."

Hannah didn't want to talk about tennis any longer. "How are you coming with your painting?"

"Fine, I guess. It's harder to paint clips and barrettes than I thought. Miss Norville says I'll be able to do it, but I wonder." Brianna pushed back her blonde hair and sighed. "It takes practice to do shadows. So does everything else!"

"But it's so much fun!"

"More fun than tennis." Brianna laughed. "I don't think tennis is our thing."

"I know, but I'm going to keep practicing. I won't give up!" She'd never give up again! Giving up was all behind her. She jumped up. "I have to go. Anytime you want to play tennis with me, let me know."

Brianna shook her head and laughed. "Thanks,

but no thanks. I thought I'd want to, but I don't. I'll stick with art."

"See you in school." Hannah waved her racket as she ran to her bike. She pedaled home, put the bike away, then stuck the racket back in the closet. "I'm home, Mom!"

"Nell phoned again," Mom called from the living room.

"Okay. I'll go see her."

"Just so you get your homework done."

"Sure, Mom." Hannah wrinkled her nose. She'd always done her homework on time. She wouldn't quit now.

A few minutes later Hannah once again opened the door to the little red barn. Heat rushed out with the smells of potting soil and sweat. Nell sat on the chair, soaking wet with perspiration. Hannah's heart plunged to her feet. "Nell!"

Nell scowled so hard, her wrinkles deepened. "Where were you?"

"Come out here where it's cooler." Hannah helped Nell stand, then walked her outdoors into the shade of a maple.

Nell dried her face with the tail of her flowered dress. Her gray hair clung damply to her head. "Why didn't you come? Your mom said you would."

"But I did! You weren't in the barn, so I went to the park. I just got back."

Nell leaned against the tree, and her eyes filled with tears. "They wouldn't let me stay at my own farm!"

"The farm belongs to someone else."

Nell jerked up. "It's mine and always will be!"

Hannah wanted to help her, but she didn't know what to say. "Maybe you could live on a farm around here."

"I don't own a farm around here!"

"I know, but there are farms outside of town. Maybe you could live there . . . or visit them. It would be better than nothing."

Nell leaned back against the tree. "Did you solve the mystery?"

"Elise did it . . . Paula's six-year-old daughter. She got mad at Paula."

Nell nodded. "I sort of had it figured that way."

Hannah quickly told her the latest news about Paula, then about joining art class and signing up for tennis and photography.

Nell frowned. "You'll be busy, won't you?"

"And I love it!" Hannah laughed breathlessly.

"You take piano too, don't you?"

Hannah nodded.

Without another word Nell walked slowly toward the house.

Hannah frowned and ran after her. "What's wrong?"

"Leave me alone. You think I got time for an Indian girl? Not me!"

Hannah froze. Indian girl? Why was Nell doing this? "Don't you even want to hear about my still-life that I'll be setting up for art?"

Nell turned at the back door and frowned. "You could paint *me*. I'm a still life—real still." She walked inside and slammed the door.

Hannah waited, hoping Nell would come back out and say she hadn't meant it. But she didn't come back.

With her head down Hannah slowly walked back to her yard.

14

The Best Friends Step In

Tuesday Hannah sat in art class and tried to listen intently to everything Miss Norville said. Hannah covered a yawn. Her mind kept flashing to Nell and why she'd suddenly turned so strange toward her.

Miss Norville walked to the front of the room and stood beside the still-life she'd set up for the class. It was a wine bottle, a block of cheese, and a chunk of bread. A lamp shone on it to give it shadows. She talked about composition and balance as she pushed her hands into the multicolored smock she wore over a purple jumpsuit. When she moved, her long, straight, red hair swung across the middle of her slender back.

Hannah leaned back in her chair. Would Nell enjoy an art class like this? Hannah frowned. Why was she thinking about Nell again? Hannah bit her lip. No matter what she'd done all day long, her mind kept going back to Nell. Several of the kids who'd been over for ice cream had given her names and addresses of farms she could check out. But why even bother? Nell only wanted her own farm.

The next day after school Hannah bent over her homework and hurried through it before going to church. Why was math so hard tonight?

Later in church she sat with the Best Friends in their special preteen group and tried to join in with the singing, but she just couldn't. Her mind wandered when Thelma Yonker taught the lesson.

After class Chelsea whispered, "Hannah, is anything wrong?"

"I guess I'm just tired tonight."

"Are you ready for the test in science tomorrow?"

Hannah shrugged. "Science is easy for me." She suddenly realized she hadn't read the rest of the chapter they'd been assigned to read. She'd do it before she went to sleep that night.

The next day in science Hannah groaned as she skipped the third question she didn't know. How was it possible that she didn't know that many answers? Her head spun, and it was hard to continue.

After school Hannah used Dad's camera and quickly took pictures of interesting things in the yard. She had planned to go to the park, but there just wasn't time. She spotted Nell and called to her. Nell turned away.

Hannah ran to her. "Can I take your picture? Please? Stand beside the barn, and I'll take it."

Nell hesitated. "Will you give me a copy?"

"Sure." Hannah stood Nell right where she wanted her, then focused the camera and clicked it. She zoomed in and took one of Nell's face just as she looked down. Her purple hat shadowed a portion of her lined face.

"Is this for the contest?"

Hannah hadn't thought about it being for the contest. She'd taken the shots just to make Nell feel less lonely. But it might make an interesting photo for the contest. "Sure. I'll enter it."

"Let me know if you win." Nell sighed. "If you think of it, that is."

"I will." Hannah hurried away. She had to take the film to be developed at a place that had one-hour service so she could hand in the photo the next day.

She rode her bike to the mall and waited while the film was developed. She looked over the photos quickly. The ones of Nell had turned out really well. The close-up would indeed be perfect for the contest. She handed the negatives of the pictures of Nell to the clerk. "Make copies of these for me please."

He nodded and put them through the process while she waited.

She paced the floor. The smell stung her nose. The noises of the mall seemed extra-loud.

Finally the copies were done. She paid for them

and pedaled home. She ran right to the red barn. The door was open, and Nell sat inside reading.

"Look!" Hannah smiled and handed Nell the photos. "I got them for you."

Nell took them and stuck them in her book without looking at them. "Don't bother me. Can't you see I'm reading?"

Tears stung Hannah's eyes. Slowly she turned and walked back home.

Friday she handed the close-up of Nell to the teacher, Mr. Scott. The corners of his brown eyes crinkled as he smiled.

"That woman has a very interesting face," he said as he studied it. "She looks lonely."

Hannah nodded. "She is. She wants to go back to her farm, but she can't."

"That's too bad." Mr. Scott stuck his fingers in the front pockets of his jeans and hunched his narrow shoulders. "She reminds me some of my grandma. She lives on a farm, but she might have to move because she's all alone."

Hannah's heart leaped. "What if she had someone live with her? What if Nell Wirt lived with her?"

Mr. Scott slowly nodded. "It's worth a shot. Give me her name, phone number, and address. I'll see that my grandma meets her so they can talk. You just might have the answer for both of them, Hannah. Nell Wirt must be very pleased to have you for a friend. It's not often that kids have time for older folks."

Hannah thought about what Mr. Scott had said again and again all day Friday. It did take time to be a friend. She knew that very well. Hmm. Just how good a friend had she been since she'd been so busy with all her extracurricular activities?

Just then she spotted the Best Friends walking down the crowded hall toward her. Why, she hadn't even had time for them like she'd had before! What kind of a friend was she? Last week she'd thought she didn't have friends any longer because the Best Friends were so busy all the time. Now she might not have friends because *she'd* become so busy!

"Hannah!" Chelsea nudged Hannah's arm. "Is it still on for tonight?"

Hannah frowned in thought. "What?"

Roxie clicked her tongue. "I told you she forgot!"

"No way," Kathy said, shaking her head. "Hannah never forgets anything."

Hannah's face flamed. The past few days she'd forgotten a lot of things.

"Pizza! The sleepover!" the Best Friends said all together.

Hannah covered her mouth. "Oh my! I did forget! And it's at *my* house! Unbelievable!" This was her very first sleepover at her house. How could she forget such an important thing? "I'm sooo sorry! Of course it's still on. Homemade pizza with Vernors and orange Slice and apple juice, of course."

"Sounds great!" Chelsea and Roxie said together.

"My mouth and my stomach are ready." Kathy laughed.

"Mom is sending the girls overnight to a friend's house, so we'll have the whole basement bedroom to ourselves." Just then Hannah remembered that she had told Brianna she'd meet her at Tandee's Art Supply Store. She told the Best Friends, and they groaned.

"I have it!" Kathy laughed. "Ask Brianna to come to the sleepover. We can all meet her at Tandee's, and she can ride her bike back with us."

Hannah nodded. "I'll do it!"

Later she found Brianna just before social studies and invited her for pizza and the sleepover.

"I'd really like to, Hannah, but I can't. If you want, we could meet at Tandee's tomorrow."

Hannah nodded. "Sure. That's fine. See ya then."

Later Hannah sat around her kitchen table with the Best Friends eating pizza. She bit off a piece, and the mozzarella cheese made a long string. She broke through the cheese with her finger and flipped the cheese back onto the pizza slice.

Chelsea drank her apple juice and set her glass

down. "We have something to say to you, Hannah. Shall we say it now or later?"

Hannah stiffened as she looked at the serious faces of the girls. "Is it really bad?"

Roxie shook her head. "Nah . . . Well, it could be."

Kathy patted Hannah's arm. "It won't hurt you, I don't think."

"Tell me now," Hannah whispered.

Chelsea leaned forward. "We all think it's great that you're doing all the extra things you're doing, but . . . we think you're doing way too much."

Hannah sank back against her chair. "Is that all?"

Chelsea nodded. "But it can get really serious, Hannah. You thought I was too busy for you, but now you're getting too busy for us . . . and for your schoolwork."

"Think about it," Kathy said softly.

"I will." Hannah slowly took another bite of pizza. She suddenly realized she had been so busy that nothing was fun—not even art.

"Well?" Roxie crossed her arms.

Chelsea and Kathy laughed. "She needs a little more time."

"I guess." Roxie took another piece of pizza and ate half of it. "Well?"

Hannah giggled. "I've been thinking the same

thing without even knowing I was thinking about it."

"I knew it," Chelsea said smugly. "I told them you'd soon realize what was happening and drop some of the things."

"I hate dropping things. It doesn't seem right."

"But it's not right to take on too much either," Kathy said. "Otherwise we'd do *everything*!"

Hannah hadn't thought about that.

"We have to choose what we want to do the most, then do *that*." Roxie leaned forward. "I won't make the tennis team, but I can have fun playing. I don't have time to practice enough to be really really good. I'd rather be really really good at carving."

"And I want to be a professional photographer someday, " Chelsea said. "So I spend a lot more time with that than most of the others do."

Hannah sighed heavily. "I know just what I'll drop. Everything but Tuesday art classes."

"But you already entered the photography contest," Chelsea said.

"I know. I'll tell Mr. Scott about my decision." Hannah's eyes widened. "I just remembered what he said today!" She quickly told them about Mr. Scott's grandma and her farm. "So he's going to get Nell and his grandma together and see what happens."

"That is sooo sweeeet!" Kathy clasped her hands together and sighed.

"But don't you mind giving up the chance to win the contest?" Chelsea asked.

Hannah thought about it a minute, then shook her head. "I like taking pictures, but I don't have the patience to get the perfect shot. It takes too much time."

"Time! Now we'll all have time to have sleep-overs and go to the mall together," Kathy said.

Suddenly Hannah thought about Nell. Now she understood why Nell was so upset with her that she wouldn't even look at her photographs! Nell knew Hannah wouldn't have time to spend with her even if she wanted to. But now she would have time—even time to visit Nell at the farm if that worked out for her.

Hannah pushed back her chair. "Girls, I'll be back in a few minutes. I have to see Nell Wirt right now."

"Is anything wrong?" they all asked together.

Hannah laughed. "Not anymore. I'll tell you about it later." And she knew they'd understand. After all, they were her best friends, and best friends always listen and understand.

You are invited to become a
Best Friends Member!

In becoming a member you'll receive a club membership card with your name on the front and a list of the Best Friends and their favorite Bible verses on the back along with a space for your favorite Scripture. You'll also receive a colorful, 2-inch, specially-made I'M A BEST FRIEND button and a write-up about the author, Hilda Stahl, with her autograph. As a bonus you'll get an occasional newsletter about the upcoming BEST FRIENDS books.

All you need to do is mail your NAME, ADDRESS (printed neatly, please), AGE and $3.00 for postage and handling to:

BEST FRIENDS
P.O. Box 96
Freeport, MI 49325

WELCOME TO THE CLUB!

(Authorized by the author, Hilda Stahl)